He's the one that we want.

"Is he coming?"

"I think you're talking about Kyle." Brianna shrugged. "*You* ask him. He hasn't said a word to me since school started. No. One word. ''Sup.' He said that. I think two days ago."

She glanced around for Kyle. Where *was* he?

"*Yo, you can't write your name over a cross-out! It's against the rules!*"

"*Hey, it's not your problem!*"

"*Is so! You gotta go to the end of the line!*"

At the head of the sign-up line, a fight was breaking out between two guys dressed in nearly identical T-shirts, rolled-up jeans, and old-school Converse basketball sneakers.

"*RUMBLE!*" shouted a girl in a pleated dress and bobby socks.

"Knock it off!" Mr. Levin cried out.

"Here we go again," Harrison said.

"DAAAARTH VADER COMMANDS YOU TO BE QUIET!" blasted through the loudspeakers.

Brianna closed her eyes.

She felt a migraine coming on.

Drama Club
Book 2:

The Big Production

Peter Lerangis

speak

An Imprint of Penguin Group (USA) Inc.

YA
FIC
LERA

SPEAK

Published by the Penguin Group
Penguin Group (USA) Inc., 345 Hudson Street, New York, New York 10014, U.S.A.
Penguin Group (Canada), 90 Eglinton Avenue East, Suite 700, Toronto, Ontario, Canada M4P 2Y3
(a division of Pearson Penguin Canada Inc.)
Penguin Books Ltd, 80 Strand, London WC2R 0RL, England
Penguin Ireland, 25 St Stephen's Green, Dublin 2, Ireland
(a division of Penguin Books Ltd)
Penguin Group (Australia), 250 Camberwell Road, Camberwell, Victoria 3124, Australia
(a division of Pearson Australia Group Pty Ltd)
Penguin Books India Pvt Ltd, 11 Community Centre,
Panchsheel Park, New Delhi - 110 017, India
Penguin Group (NZ), 67 Apollo Drive, Rosedale, North Shore 0745, Auckland, New Zealand
(a division of Pearson New Zealand Ltd.)
Penguin Books (South Africa) (Pty) Ltd, 24 Sturdee Avenue,
Rosebank, Johannesburg 2196, South Africa

Registered Offices: Penguin Books Ltd, 80 Strand, London WC2R 0RL, England

Published by Speak, an imprint of Penguin Group (USA) Inc., 2007

1 3 5 7 9 10 8 6 4 2

LIBRARY OF CONGRESS CATALOGING-IN-PUBLICATION DATA

Lerangis, Peter.
Drama club 2 : the big production / Peter Lerangis.
p. cm.
ISBN 978-0-14-240887-2
1. High school students—Fiction. 2. Acting—Fiction. I. Title. II. Title: Drama club two.
PS3569.I5257D733 2007   813'.54—dc22   2007015355

Speak ISBN 978-0-14-240887-2

Printed in the United States of America

Prologue

IVY'S

The Gospel According to Brianna Glaser

In the beginning there was the Word.
And the Light.
And the Music.
And when they were put together
When people said the Word
And looked into the Light
And danced to the Music
There was chaos.
And so God created the Director and the Stage Manager
and the Musical Director and the Choreographer.
And on the seventh day THERE WAS A CAST PARTY.

FROM THE SEA

S51. Shrimp with tofu and bok choy with Ma-La Sauce.....................8.95

Suculant jumbo shrimps with secial tangy sauce. Mild, medium or spicey.

I was in a religious mood when I wrote that. I'm not usually that way. Especially at a cast party. Especially while looking at the menu at Ivy's Chinese Café. Well, okay, *ever*. (My mom's Presbyterian and my dad's Jewish, so I grew up in the Church of Confusion.)

Blame it on *Godspell*.

It was our fall production. You probably know already, but *Godspell* is this seventies musical where Jesus and his disciples sing and dance in clown costumes. I was the assistant director. Also I took over for the lead girl just hours before the show, with no rehearsal. And I didn't suck.

Not sucking would seem a modest goal under normal circumstances, but not here at Ridgeport High. When it comes to musicals, we're kind of a warp world. Enter the front door and you see all the usual stuff—green tile walls, kids with iPods, trophy cases, old photos. But the kids are listening to *Avenue Q* and *Rent*, and the photos are of the casts of school plays dating back to 1907. We have pep rallies to raise money for the Drama Club. Five of our alums have won Tony Awards for best performances on Broadway. The *New York Times* wrote about us. They said high school theater in Ridgeport was like high school football in Texas. No doubt. At Ridgeport, the sports teams complain that the drama kids get too much attention.

Btw, we *do* have a football team. They're pretty good, from what I hear. They generally don't do theater. Except for one of them. Kyle Taggart.

I plucked him from obscurity and made him try out. And he was a big reason that I did not suck in *Godspell*.

Some actors have to work hard to shine; others steal the

limelight just stepping on the stage. But once in a while you see someone so good, so natural, that they make everyone else look like stars, too. That's Kyle. I heard him singing at a party and forced him to audition. He had no experience. But when he stepped on the stage, you couldn't take your eyes off him. So we cast him as Jesus. He was perfect. It didn't hurt that he was a hottie and had killer high notes. Everyone loved him.

Kyle was very much like his character. He Loved Them All Back. Equally. Which meant that at any given time, depending on whom he was with, the rest of Them All were really pissed at him.

The Getting of Kyle was the drama within the drama. Yes, I was drawn into it, too. But not too deeply. I'm way too careful for that. By the time of the cast party at Ivy's, I had already checked out of that particular Heartbreak Hotel. Or so I thought.

I stuck with this sensible decision right into winter break. Which wasn't really a break, what with SAT prep, essay tutoring, studying ahead to avoid falling behind during Spring Musical rehearsals, and college visits to Yale and Harvard.

As my dad says, "This is junior year, Bunky." Don't ask me why he says Bunky. He says it like it's supposed to be funny. I guess his students laugh, but I imagine college students laugh at whatever the professor finds funny.

My friends think I'm obsessive. I don't buy that. I was brought up to do my best at everything. Consider the source. My dad is not only a business professor but a natural-history expert. The kind of guy who's proud to have a stuffed collared peccary (that's like a small hog) named George on our mantel. Mom runs a hedge fund and plays classical piano. In my family, if you *don't* go to Yale or Harvard, there must be something wrong with you.

So during that winter break, while everyone else was traveling into the city to see "the tree" and singing carols and Netflixing *It's a Wonderful Life* and *Scrooged*, I was augmenting a copiously fecund vocabulary, wrestling with the quadratic equation, wondering in my spare time about which play would be chosen for the big Spring Musical, and worrying whether I would be allowed to play a lead role, considering I'd played one in *Godspell*. (In my favor: [a] We had never done a small Fall Musical like *Godspell* before, so there was no precedent for a no-lead-role-twice rule, and [b] I didn't exactly ask for that lead, it was thrust upon me.)

Plus, someone hacked the school computer and found out that Caleb Deutsch's GPA was .007 points higher than mine, and he was first in the class.

These were the things keeping me up at night. I don't even remember what I got for Christmas. Ho ho ho. I was not a happy camper.

And then, on a cold December evening, Jesus asked me to meet him at the beach.

Naturally I said yes.

Part 1
All Shook Up

December 29

1

"HOW FAR?" KYLE SAID, LIFTING A BEACH UMBRELLA pole off the sand.

Brianna tried to smile but her teeth were chattering. It had to be below freezing. She hadn't noticed it as much when he'd had his arms around her, when they were walking. Kyle gave off a lot of heat and didn't seem to feel the temperature. He was wearing an RHS football-team sweatshirt with cut-off sleeves, and dark blue gym shorts. "How far *what*? You're going to throw that thing? I don't know . . . three miles."

Kyle balanced the pole and looked toward the jetty, which snaked into the water and looked like a distant serpent in the moonlight. "Come on," he said. "Seriously."

"*I don't know.* Just don't kill any s-s-seagulls," Brianna replied.

It.

Is.

Not.

COLD.

Brianna negotiated with her brain. *You agreed to be here,* she told it. *Think of the sand. The moon. The splashing waves.*

The cold, her brain replied. *Cold. Cold. Cold. Cold. Cold. Cold.*

She watched him draw back the stupid pole. It was made of wood, pointed at the forward end and with a band of metal circling the other, where the umbrella fabric had once been attached.

"Over the sign," he said, which Brianna took to be a prediction that he would throw the thing over a wooden sign that read WARNING: IT IS ILLEGAL TO CLIMB UPON OR WALK ON THE JETTY WITHOUT THE PRESENCE OF A LIFEGUARD.

And the first thought in Brianna's mind—peeking out from her shivery, wretched thoughts of the cold—was not *What is wrong with this picture?* or *Who IS this jerk?* but this: *If the throw arcs at amplitude* x, *where the release point is defined as (0,0), and it travels at a speed of* q *feet per second for* t *seconds, then what is the formula for the parabola?*

Oh God.

February 23. Less than two months, and the SAT would be over.

Kyle ran a few steps, his bare feet digging into the sand, his body tilted right. With his flowing hair and chiseled arms, he looked like a figure on a Grecian urn, only with more clothes. *"Heeeaaargh!"* he cried as he lurched forward, hurling the pole.

Brianna watched the pole sail high into the darkness. "If you do that at some gyms, they kick you out."

"Throw an umbrella?" Kyle asked.

"No, grunt," Brianna replied. "I saw it on the news."

"Really? That sucks."

A thump sounded in the distance. "Damn. Off to the right." Kyle was jumping now, looking down at his feet.

"You're cold?" Brianna said hopefully. "Finally?"

"No. Why?"

"You're jumping."

Kyle shrugged. "I'm testing Arthur. No pain. The sand is good for him."

"Arthur?"

"My ankle," he said with a smile, holding up the ankle that changed the world. The ankle whose injury caused him to drop off the football team, thereby allowing him to try out for *Godspell*. "*You're* the one who made up the name."

Brianna looked at him curiously. "Um . . . no . . . "

"Wait. Crap. That was Reese."

Ouch.

Mistaking her for Reese Van Cleve? During this masochistic weather ordeal? After she had sacrificed her health to come all the way out here, *to watch him throw an umbrella pole*? "Yes, well, people often confuse us. You know, blond and overachieving me . . . red-haired and slutty her . . . "

"Sorry!" Kyle sputtered. "I didn't mean—"

Brianna turned back toward the boardwalk. "Does Reese have nicknames for any other parts of your body?" she said over her shoulder. "Billy the bicep . . . Timmy the tush? Ooh, how's little Petey doing?"

"Wait!" Kyle jogged to catch up with her. "Where are you going?"

"Home," Brianna replied. "In my car. Alone."

"You can't do that!" Kyle insisted.

"Why not? Arthur will take care of you. And Larry the leg."

"It's six miles!" He raced past her, grabbing her shoulder bag. "I have your keeeys . . . "

Brianna lunged toward him, trying to snatch back the bag. "Dude? My bag is not a football."

He jumped onto the boardwalk and ran behind a large wooden bulletin board. Sticking his head out from behind the board, he dangled the keys. "What are you going to give me for them?"

"This." Brianna reared back and kicked under the sign. But Kyle was quick. He stepped aside, and Brianna's shin made contact with the bottom edge. "Yeeooow! Damn it, Kyle, that hurt!"

She turned away, limping. Very convincingly, too. Sometimes acting skills came in handy.

Now he was around the sign, standing in front of her, a look of concern on his face. "Sorry." He put an arm around her and guided her to a bench.

Brianna snatched the bag back. "I can walk on my own."

"Nice trick," he said, leaning closer. "Good kick, too. I think you broke the wood. Hey, the football team needs a punter . . ."

It was a lame line. But she could think of worse things than his big comfy body drawing close on a night like this. His breath was warm and slightly sweet, like a breakfast pastry.

And just like that, without thinking—because these kinds of things never involved thinking, because if she *had* thought about it and weighed the pros and cons, she would have said no—just like that, their faces were together. And he didn't taste like a pastry. He tasted intoxicating like the ocean, limitless and scary like the winter sky.

She knew this was a bad idea. This vacation was supposed to be about other things. Definitely not Kyle. She had already spent too much quality time on Kyle during *Godspell*, thinking about him, loving and hating him, wrapping her mind around the concept of how he fit into her life—which, she had finally decided, was not very much.

But the parabolas in her mind were gone, the multiple choices and analogies had wicked away into the starry night, and it all felt nice. Playful. Like they had just finished a scene from a goofy Jennifer Aniston comedy.

"Hmm," she said.

"Cold?" He wrapped her in bare arms. He was warmer than down.

"This isn't real, you know . . . " Brianna said.

"It isn't?" Kyle asked. "Then what is it?"

Brianna shrugged. "I don't know—a movie? A play?"

"Act One. Fight ends. Curtain."

"What do we do for Act Two?" Brianna asked.

Kyle smiled. "Something crazy."

"Like . . . ?"

"Well, we can't do it here."

"So think of something else."

His eyes darted to the billboard. "Bingo."

POLAR BEAR CLUB
NEW YEAR'S SUNRISE SWIM
JONES BEACH FIELD 3
JANUARY 1
FOLLOWED BY BARBECUE

"God, you are so romantic," Brianna said drily.

Kyle stood up, pulling her to her feet. "Come on."

"Come on *what*?"

"Let's be Polar Bears."

"You're not *serious*? Those are the guys who go in the *water*, Kyle. In the winter."

He was pulling off his sweatshirt. "Chicken?"

"*Chicken*?" Brianna said. "No one says *chicken*. Kyle, are you feeling okay? Do I, like, *know* you?"

"You will now!" He reached for her arm but she backed away.

He was bare-chested now. His torso was ripped. Six-pack abs, shoulders like loaves of bread. Chuckie the chest. Percy and Paul the pecs. With a shrug, he began sliding his shorts down.

"Kyle, you are not going to do this!"

"No one's here."

"No one? What do you mean, no one—?"

He turned to the ocean and began to run. In seconds, he disappeared into the darkness, calling out, "Come on!"

"You are crazy!"

An impossibly loud *"GEEUUUUHHH!"* bellowed from the sea as Kyle hit the surf. It didn't sound like Kyle at all. It didn't sound human.

Doing this was not human.

What if he had a heart attack and died?

Brianna ran toward the water. She couldn't see him. She couldn't hear a thing.

He was dead. The shock had killed him. The undertow was already pulling his dead body out to sea. "Ky-y-yle, you jackass, where are you!"

She tripped over something that wrapped itself around her ankle. Kyle's gym shorts and underwear. Torn off at the last minute before jumping in.

No answer. She could see the headlines: RIDGEPORT HIGH FOOTBALL STAR DIES NAKED ON BEACH WITH GIRLFRIEND. "KY-Y-Y-YLE!" she cried out.

Then she heard a splashing sound.

Chup . . . chup . . . chup . . . swooosh . . .

Swimming. To her left.

A shadow rose from the water like a strange beast, the silhouette black in the moonlight. Kyle was out now, running toward her, moving fast. Even in the dark she could see him shiver. "Wow! WOO-HOOO!" he cried out.

"I don't believe this," Brianna said.

"Dude! Th-th-that w-w-was so COOL! It totally makes you f-f-feel amazing! Like n-n-nothing else in the world matters! Try it!"

"Don't you dare touch me I am FREEZING, Kyle."

He kept running, whooping, laughing, every muscle tensed with the cold. Jumping up and down. Dripping and stark naked. Hysterical. Elated like a five-year-old. Like her obnoxious little brother, Colter, only bigger and hairier. And now he was heading straight for his clothes, which would take him right past her.

What did he want? What was this all about?

Did he know? Did he even care?

Oh God, leering is so not cool.

As he passed, she turned her eyes away.

Sort of.

2

BEE-DOOP.

At the sound of the incoming IM, Brianna's elbow slid off her desk. Her head, which had been carefully propped on her wrists, dropped. Jarred by the movement, she caught herself before the possibility of jaw damage.

She blinked awake, out of a dream. In it, she had been standing in a long hallway echoing with monkey screeches. At the end of the hall was the Yale dorm room that belonged to her best friend, Rachel Kolodzny, who was last year's Drama Club stage manager. But the door was made of metal bars, and inside the room Rachel was shouting *Jail, not Yale!*, laughing and laughing and laughing . . .

YaLeBiRd: *yo bri, ru still up?*

dramakween: i was just thinking of you. this is so weird.

YaLeBiRd: *psychic*

dramakween: more like psycho. i must have fallen asleep, you were in jail.

YaLeBiRd: *that's what I feel like. i have finals. hellllppppp*

dramakween: don't complain, i wish i were at yale instead of seating it out here

YaLeBiRd: *seating?*

dramakween: sweating. dont be picky. rach, i cant stay awake or concentrate. i was on the beach tonight with kt & he was naked

YaLeBiRd: *u were getting jiggy with the jock?*

dramakween: hahaha. i dont understand him, he just took off his clothes and went swimming , it wasnt sexual or anything or maybe it was SUPPOSED to be but im really not into him

YaLeBiRd: *invite me next time. no one at yale looks like THAT*

dramakween: point is i need to be studying. i did not need this distraction. kt, I mean. i'm supposed to be like remembering about asymptotes and secants, and now all i think about are 2 things—kt (what was THAT all about?) and drama club and what musical we're gonna do cuz the suspense is KILLING ME

YaLeBiRd: *mr levin hasn't made up his mind yet for spring musical????*

dramakween: NO!!!!! . . .

dramakween: i swear rach, i am gonna flunk the sats like get a 600 and there goes yale down the toilet

YaLeBiRd: whoa

dramakween: cuz i'll b washing dishes at kostas korner with all the greek waiters staring at my clevage

YaLeBiRd: cleavage

dramakween: i cant even spell!!!!!!

YaLeBiRd: hey that was a joke

YaLeBiRd: um . . . reality check . . .

YaLeBiRd: 2 yrs ago i was just like u? remember? convinced i was gonna flunk? forgetting everything?

dramakween: u were valedictorian. plus the best stage manager ever btw

YaLeBiRd: i forgot the doghouse cue in "charlie brown" and snoopy had to lie on the floor

YaLeBiRd: i threw up when yale deferred me after i applied early acceptance

YaLeBiRd: Look, wum sayin is . . . ive been there. u just need a vacation

dramakween: i just HAD one! i cant help this . . .

dramakween: rach, seriously, what if they pick a sucky play?

YaLeBiRd: there are no sucky plays, just sucky actors ☺

dramakween: RU SAYING I SUCK?

YaLeBiRd: NO!!! oy. get some sleep, brianna

dramakween: u sound like mom

YaLeBiRd: and brush yr teeth young lady ☺

• • •

"ARE WE ALL HERE?" shouted Harrison Michaels, barging into the vaulted cavern known as the Murray Klein Memorial Auditorium.

Brianna dropped her messenger bag onto a seat. "Dashiell's missing," she said. "Probably up in the booth doing his tech thing."

Reese Van Cleve, the Drama Club choreographer, lowered herself to a full split on the center aisle, arching her back so that the top of her head touched the carpet. "I'm here, Mr. President," she said. "And I am dying to know what musical we're doing."

"Don't know yet, Reese." Harrison set a big bag of pastries—a donation from his dad's diner—on the edge of the stage.

"Does your vice know?" Reese asked.

"Vice *president*," Brianna grumbled. She was in no mood for Reese's humor.

"What smells so insanely good?" Casey Chang, the Drama Club's stage manager, peeked out from behind the curtains, her dark eyes coming to rest on the bag. "Your dad is trying to make us fat again," she moaned. "And I lost seven pounds over break."

"Charles loves this stuff," Harrison said. "Where is he?"

"Call out 'Genius Set and Costume Designer!'" Reese advised. "That usually works."

"People, what are you doing out here?" said Charles Scopetta, skipping onto the stage through a door in the back wall. "Come look at our new Green Room! I *love* our Green Room!"

Brianna smiled. She thought she had forgotten how to

smile. It was the first smile since the Night of the Living Kyle. Which seemed now like the Night That Never Happened. Okay, it was only the first day back since the end of winter break. But every time she had seen Kyle today, he acted as if he had amnesia. Maybe the whole thing had been some kind of *Lost* flashback.

Charles was the only person who could lift her mood from dismal to just below sour in three seconds flat. "I hate green," she said.

"That's because you are just *so* stunning, darling, that *every* room turns green when you enter," Charles replied, taking her by the hand. "Come. See."

Brianna climbed the stage along with the other Drama Club members. On the back wall, which until now had been solid, a door opened into a huge, freshly painted room. "For years, a dingy computer room . . . unloved, unused," Charles announced. "And now, thanks to the magic of our enchanting janitor, Mr. Hortensio Ippolito, who single-handedly banished the old equipment, renovated the space, and punched a door through the wall using nothing but his fists, Ridgeport has what it has always needed—a place for gathering, putting on costumes and makeup, bitching, moaning, and otherwise being a Drama Club—*a Green Room!*"

"Hortensio?" said Harrison.

Charles shrugged. "I made it up. It's Shakespearean, yet somehow contemporary. What is Mr. Ippolito's name, anyway?"

"Cosmo?" Brianna said.

"I thought it was Rudy," said Casey.

"Come away, people." Charles steered them out of the Green Room. "The paint is still wet. And remember, today we start planning the Spring Musical."

"We don't even know what it is yet," said Casey, heading downstage.

"Mr. Levin and Ms. Gunderson are fighting it out," Harrison explained, extracting a Tupperware container of pastries from the paper bag. "Happy holidays. Galactobouriko for all. . . ."

"God, that sounds sexy." Reese licked her lips suggestively.

"It's phyllo dough and custard, Reese." Harrison held one out to her.

"No thanks," Reese replied. "My thighs have suffered enough over the vacation."

"Darling, please, we can only imagine where your thighs have been during winter break," said Charles.

"Charles!" Reese said.

Charles examined Harrison's offering. His swooping brown hair fell over his eyes. The hair, as well as his waistline, had grown over the vacation. "Well, I'll sacrifice," he said, lifting a gooey pastry. "The diet begins mañana. Unless we pick *South Pacific*. In which case I will not need a diet, as I will be running halfway across the county at the thought of having to make costumes out of palm fronds and coconuts. Mmmmmm . . . tastes fresh."

"It's a day old," Harrison replied. "The new manager at the diner was throwing it out with the chicken carcasses."

"You really know how to sell it . . . " Charles said with a grimace.

Suddenly the houselights began to flicker. A bizarre mechanical voice called over the loudspeaker. "LU-U-U-U-UKE I AM YOUR FA-A-A-ATHER . . . " *BRRRRACKK!*

"Um, what was *that?*" Casey called over her shoulder.

Dashiell Hawkins's face popped into the window of the projection booth. He was bony and handsome with chocolate-brown skin, his large eyes overwhelming the narrow black frame of his glasses, which were constantly slipping down his nose. "A vocoder. I got it on eBay. I believe it has a few bugs. That was Darth—could you tell?"

The auditorium door flew open. Mr. Levin, the faculty adviser, rushed in with an armful of papers. He looked tan and fit, much more relaxed than he had been after *Godspell.* It was easy to imagine him as the Broadway actor he once was. His beard was highlighted so intensely with red that Brianna wondered if he had spent time in the sun or with the good folks at Clairol. "Happy New Year, everyone!" he cried out.

Behind him, smiling and chipper, was the Drama Club musical supervisor, Ms. Gunderson. Her hair was golden white, pulled back in a black headband, and it bounced as she waved cheerily to everyone. From the crisp pleats of her plaid skirt to the vivid white turtleneck blouse, it looked as though she had once again had a fruitful L.L. Bean Christmas.

"Check out the grin," murmured Reese. "I think they finally did it."

"On some tropical island," Harrison said.

"With palm fronds and coconuts," Charles said under his breath, politely waving to the two teachers. "Oh, the visions that dance in my head . . ."

"Welcome back, everyone!" Mr. Levin announced as he sat on the lip of the stage. "As you know, Ms. Gunderson and I have had long talks with all of you over the break about which musical we should do. And we had a *lot* of different opinions . . ."

"Did you get my technical analysis?" called Dashiell, who was running down from the booth. "Of *Sweeney Todd*? It was a pdf attachment—"

"*Sweeney*, alas, is out," Mr. Levin said. "Too bloody."

"Imagine the cleanup," Harrison added. "The Charlettes would faint."

"We discussed it, though," Ms. Gunderson said, "and we discussed Reese's suggestion of *Hair*."

"Of course! There's a nude scene," Charles said. "Reese could do it as a solo."

Reese reached over and slapped Charles's shoulder.

" . . . But Ms. Gunderson and I have reached a decision," Mr. Levin said, "after a long discussion . . ."

"Deep into the night . . ." Reese whispered.

"Wait! Wait! I would like to be present at the unveiling!" Dashiell sprinted the last few yards down the aisle. He took a seat next to Brianna. She put her arm around him. Charles put his arm around her.

"This year's Spring Musical," Ms. Gunderson said with a sly glint, "will be *Grease*."

"*Grease*?" said Casey.

"Unexpected, but intriguing," Dashiell remarked.

"Yyyyessss!" Charles blurted out. "I'm in heaven."

"You are?" Harrison said.

"Leather jackets, bobby socks, big hair, a hot rod on stage? What's not to like?" Charles said.

"Jitterbugging, throws . . . " Reese said. "Sweet."

"I'll look into the lighting opportunities," Dashiell added.

"I think we can convince Peter Mansfield to be the student musical director," Ms. Gunderson said. "He's a nut for this type of music."

"You mean Schroeder?" Reese said.

Brianna smiled, remembering Peter's role in a summer production of *You're a Good Man, Charlie Brown*. He was a shy, bookish guy, not much of an actor, but a kick-ass musician.

"He studied piano with me for years," Ms. Gunderson said proudly. "He's starting the Juilliard weekend program next year."

Harrison shifted heavily in his seat. "I wasn't expecting *Grease*," he said to Brianna.

"Not serious enough for you?" she said softly. "Mr. All-Sondheim-All-the-Time?"

"It's a nice big cast," Mr. Levin explained. "The Drama Club hasn't done it in twenty-three years—"

"And Mr. Levin was in it on Broadway," Ms. Gunderson piped up.

"I was in the national tour," Mr. Levin said, blushing. "Well, one of them. I understudied the part of Doody."

"We could have a fifties dance in the school for a fundraiser," Casey suggested.

"*Grease* is a seventies show, you know," Harrison said. "A seventies spoof of the fifties. With music that's supposed to sound kind of cheesy and derivative and uninteresting."

"This is what I like about you, Harrison," Charles said. "So full of fun and fizz."

Brianna watched Harrison trying to laugh off Charles's comment. Harrison was a terrific actor, maybe one of the best Ridgeport ever had. He could do Shakespeare and make you cry. His accents were perfect. He was handsome in an intense, brooding way, *and* he could do comedy. But he wasn't *that* good when it came to hiding his distaste for something. *Grease* was not a Harrison Michaels kind of a show. The lead role, Danny Zuko, was hunky and dim. Hunky and dim did not turn Harrison on.

"Eugene is a really good character part," Brianna said. "Or Kenickie, the best friend? The bad boy? That's the part I'd want if I were you, Harrison."

"Exactly. Totally," Harrison said. "Thanks."

"Ooooh, do I hear a little hissy fit?" Reese said.

"Sssssss," said Harrison, returning to his galactobouriko.

When he was out of earshot, Reese whispered to Brianna, "He's worried about a replay of *Godspell*."

"Replay?" Brianna said.

"Well, duh. We know the real reason they picked *Grease*. I won't mention any names, but there is one person in this school born to play Danny Zuko. And you know who it is."

"I *don't* know, Reese," Brianna said.

"Polar Bear Boy," Reese said, heading toward the stage. "The naked swimmer."

Brianna seized up inside. How did Reese *know*? "I—I'm not following . . ."

"Oh, please. Don't act so surprised," Reese said with a laugh. "You and Kyle? Hooking up on the beach? It's the talk of the school."

3

"UH-HUH, BABY, YEOOWW, GET OFF MY SHOES..."

No. That didn't sound right. Or look right.

Keep the jaw loose. Eyes at half-mast.

Harrison squirted some more gel into his hands, rubbed it into his hair, and combed it up into a perfect ducktail. The Saturday lunch was light today, so he might as well use the time. Auditions were close—two days away—and he needed all the practice he could get.

Too smart, he thought, judging the look on his own face in the mirror. That was the problem. He shut his eyes just a bit, like his lids were too heavy. He let his mouth hang open.

There.

Mr. Levin was right. Add those two facial adjustments,

subtract twenty IQ points. Now for the voice. Lower pitch, slower speech.

"Uh, ladies 'n' genlmun, uh, thankyuh vurry much . . . "

BOOM.

The door opened, smacking against the bathroom wall.

"WHERE IS THE PASTITSIO ON TABLE TWO?"

Harrison spun around to face his father, whose broad frame nearly touched both sides of the door. Kostas Michalakis, aka Kostas Michaels of Kostas Korner (Gus, to some of his pronunciation-challenged friends), was beloved for his jolly laugh, his ability to remember everyone's name, and the quick service at his diner.

But there was a price to pay for all that popularity. He was a tough guy to work for. Especially if you were his son.

"Wull, I dunno, Daddy-o," Harrison said. "Ask Niko. He's da waiter. I'm da busboy, thankyuh vurry much . . . "

"Why you talk like that?" his father said. "You don't hear Yiorgo in the kitchen? He say, 'The pastitsio is ready!' and nobody answer. You have to comb the hair and make the faces in the mirror, not help Niko? You supposed to be bus*boy*! Not *girl*!"

"Ooh, yuh call me a girl, make fun-a muh face, put me to work all ovuh the place—"

"HARALAMBOS—"

"Jes' don' drop pastitsio on muh blue suede shoes-ah!" Harrison said, rushing past him and into the kitchen.

"AND TAKE THE CIGARETTES OUT OF YOU SHIRT!"

Harrison took the pack of candy cigs from his rolled-up shirtsleeve, crammed them into his pocket, and quickly pulled the sleeve down. Behind the kitchen serving counter, George the chef was cracking up. "Wassup, Elvis?"

Harrison grabbed the pastitsio and put it on a tray. "Thankyuh vurry much . . ."

"Don't forget the side dish," George said.

Turning back, Harrison grabbed a hot plate full of crisp green broccoli and headed out the swinging kitchen door, just as Niko, the waiter, headed in.

The thick wooden door could not muffle the sound of his father's voice: "NIKO, WHY YOU SO SLOW? MY SON IS DOING YOU JOB AND HE'S ONLY A KID!"

Harrison rushed into the diner and headed for table 3.

Away from the war zone.

4

!!TODAY!!

JAN. 14

THIS IS IT!!

AUDITIONS
FOR THE ANNUAL RIDGEPORT HIGH
DRAMA CLUB SPRING MUSICAL,

GREASE!

3:45 IN THE AUDITORIUM
BE THERE OR BE SQUARE!

*EXTRA DAY OF AUDITIONS ANNOUNCED
FOR TOMORROW FOR OVERFLOW!*

Brianna had expected a mob. The Spring Musical always brought out everybody, sometimes even people you never saw before.

But this was worse than usual. Bruce Hansen and Ilya Zedlovich had already been kicked off the line by Mr. Levin for fighting. The line had to be split into two, and both Charles and Casey were madly answering questions and signing people up for audition slots.

Already Mr. Levin had authorized another day of auditions, just to accommodate the high turnout.

"Keep it moving!" Brianna said. "Ask your questions now. Don't wait till you get to the sheet!"

"She-bop she-bam, ramalama bing bong," said Royce Reardon, combing back his black, greased-back hair with a flourish of his right arm.

"Thank you for signing," Charles was saying for the hundredth time. "Would you like to be considered for the Charlettes, Ridgeport's award-winning backstage team?"

For a split second, Brianna spotted Harrison talking on his cell phone, pacing the lobby and gesturing. But he was immediately blocked from view by Jenny Koh, a sophomore who was on the robotics team. "Do we have to have the song memorized?"

"No, you can hold the music or a lyric sheet," Brianna replied. "Just make sure Ms. Gunderson has a copy of the music."

"Or Peter Mansfield," piped up a voice from behind her. With a shy grin, Peter the piano genius smiled as he headed toward the piano. He had a round face, a Dutch-boy haircut, and a wardrobe direct from Lacoste.

Over and over, Brianna answered the same questions—how many bars do we get to sing *(anywhere from sixteen to a whole verse, no one's strictly counting)*, do we need to be in costume *(no)*, when are callbacks *(Friday)*, what if you don't reach my spot by the end of today's audition *(come back tomorrow)*, etc., etc. She hugged each *Godspell* cast member who showed up—Ethan Smith, Corbin Smythe, Jamil Moore, Lynnette Freeman, Aisha Rashid—even Lori Terrell, the amazing singer who had dropped out of *Godspell* because of her parents' religious objections. Lori wasn't going to audition for *Grease* because it conflicted with a concert she was performing in—but she was full of apologies and Brianna was full of forgiveness. That's the way these things went.

By the time Harrison barged his way back into the auditorium, the chaos had died down. "Sorry about that," he said. "Dad wanted me to come in to teach Guillermo about the sidework. I told him no."

"Guillermo?" Brianna asked.

"The new manager of the diner," Harrison replied, scanning the throng, nodding to various people. "Hey, what's Dino Testaverde doing here? He hates the DC. And so does Cooper Wallace, the Goth Shadow. Jenny Koh . . . Chip Duggan? Half the Engineering Club. The Speech and Debate Team. Those guys never show up. This is mad crazy!"

"You seem perky," Brianna said, "for someone who hates *Grease*."

"My ancestors were born there," Harrison replied. "Thankyuh vurry much . . ."

Brianna groaned. Harrison was slipping into character. And the character was most likely Danny Zuko, although it needed work. Zuko didn't make bad jokes.

"One guy I *don't* see is your boyfriend the jock," Harrison continued.

"I'll let that comment pass on account of cluelessness, which you can't help."

"Is he coming?"

"I think you're talking about Kyle." Brianna shrugged. "*You* ask him. He hasn't said a word to me since school started. No. One word. ''Sup.' He said that. I think two days ago."

She glanced around for Kyle. Where *was* he?

"*Yo, you can't write your name over a cross-out! It's against the rules!*"

"*Hey, it's not your problem!*"

"*Is so! You gotta go to the end of the line!*"

At the head of the sign-up line, a fight was breaking out between two guys dressed in nearly identical T-shirts, rolled-up jeans, and old-school Converse basketball sneakers.

"*RUMBLE!*" shouted a girl in a pleated dress and bobby socks.

"Knock it off!" Mr. Levin cried out.

"Here we go again," Harrison said.

"DAAAARTH VADER COMMANDS YOU TO BE QUIET!" blasted through the loudspeakers.

Brianna closed her eyes.

She felt a migraine coming on.

• • •

"Brianna? *Brianna, wake up!*"

Brianna leaped in her seat, fresh out of a dream. A bad dream. Taking place at Yale. In Rachel Kolodzny's dorm room. Rachel was there—along with Kyle and Brianna's parents. And a long umbrella. It all fit somehow. But the details evaporated into the air the moment she banged her knee on the armrest. "Ow! What?"

"They just called your name!"

Casey was standing over her, with a familiar look of quiet freak-out. Brianna checked the auditorium clock: 5:23. She had been asleep for ten minutes. Her clipboard, filled with her own observations of other people's auditions, lay on the carpeted floor. As Drama Club vice president, she was supposed to judge each auditioner. Except herself.

"Am I next?" she asked.

"You're on deck, after Simone Frechette," Casey replied.

"Oh, say, can you seeeeeee . . ." warbled Simone, standing center stage in a major body slump with her angle-cut hair across her eyes.

So far today it was the sixth "Star-Spangled Banner." That was the suggested song for anyone who didn't have one prepared.

Across her evaluation sheet, Brianna wrote:

Hello? Clue?

Casey cringed. "Ouch."

"This is a *show*. People are supposed to come prepared." Brianna took a deep breath and closed her eyes. "Sorry.

Sorry. I'm always grouchy when I wake up. But thanks, Casey."

"Break a leg, diva," Casey said with a smile before rushing off.

Brianna rose from her seat and turned her back to the stage. Quickly, quietly, she did a focusing exercise taught to her by a vocal coach her dad knew. It was a set of moves that involved looking at your palms in front of your eyes. She didn't know why it worked, but it did.

From the third row of seats, Mr. Levin said, "Thank you, Simone. Callbacks will be Friday, and names will be posted Friday morning! Next—Brianna?"

"Magic time," Brianna muttered to herself.

She smoothed the pleats of the white skirt she had found in the thrift shop. Gathering her hair, she pulled it back into a ponytail and thought about the exercises she had done over the weekend.

Physical life—she bounced as she walked, a friendly, cheerleader bounce that worked for her character, Sandy Dumbrowski.

Sense memory—she saw the world through Sandy's eyes. The auditorium was neat. Everyone was so nice. How cute Charles was! And Simone was such a trooper.

"Nice job," she said as she passed Simone.

"Right," Simone replied with a sneer. "Like this is so fair. Like you even *have* to audition."

Brianna spun around. "What—?"

But Simone was headed up the aisle, walking fast.

"*That* was snarky," Charles said.

Brianna nodded. But her concentration was broken.

The part of her that was Sandy wanted to cry; the part that was Brianna wanted to run after Simone and throttle her.

Shut it out. Shut it all out. Stay in the moment.

In character.

"Hi, Ms. Gunderson!" she chirped, approaching the piano. "Hi, Peter Mansfield! Here's my music. Have a nice day."

Ms. Gunderson cracked up.

Great. She wasn't supposed to do that. It wasn't a comedy role. She was going too far.

Brianna handed over her sheet music and jumped onto the stage. "Whenever you're ready," she said politely.

The opening notes of "Mister Postman" sounded. Brianna started to sing.

No. No no no no.

She was flat. Sharp. One or the other. She couldn't tell. But it just sounded wrong. Her voice was filling the auditorium in some whacked-out key.

Brianna smiled. A Sandy smile. An oops-I'm-doing-this-on-purpose-because-I'm-really-a-modest-girl smile. When you're desperate, pretend you meant to do it.

And now there was *snickering* in the back of the auditorium. Simone and her friends, peering in from the hallway.

"Will someone shut that door, please!" Harrison called out.

"Shoo!" Charles scolded, running toward them.

Peter stopped playing. "Let's start again," he said.

"Sure," Brianna said, but the word caught in her throat and came out sounding more like "Shuck."

"Just relax, sweetie," Ms. Gunderson said.

Oh God. *Relax?* That was what you said to other kids. The shy kids. The incompetent ones. You told *them* to relax.

What was happening?

Brianna tried to smile. Her lips were shaking. She *never* felt like this.

They were all staring at her. Reese, Harrison, Dashiell, Charles, Casey.

Her knees shook.

And now the music was starting again. Brianna loosened her fingers, which were balled into fists. She looked to the back of the auditorium, focusing on a spot on the wall. She felt a drop of sweat plink onto her cheek from her brow. *Flop sweat.*

She opened her mouth to sing.

And she prayed.

5

DAY TWO OF AUDITIONS. HARRISON LOOKED AT HIS watch and then up at Reese, who was leaping across the stage to the tune of "All That Jazz," all kicks and thrusts and pouty looks.

"Nice, Reese, thank you!" Harrison called out.

Great kicks, but this is GREASE, *not* CHICAGO, he wrote on his eval sheet.

He knew Reese would see that. It would upset her. It was fun to upset Reese. She was upsettable. "Next . . . Devon Roper!"

Harrison glanced at Dashiell in the next seat, who was deep into an Autocad printout of something that was either an electrical grid or a map of the human brain. "Is *upsettable* a word?" Harrison asked. Besides being their tech guru, Dashiell was a walking dictionary.

"I believe not," Dashiell said.

"Upsetworthy?" Harrison pressed.

Dashiell shook his head. "Negatory."

Brianna would know. He turned toward the back of the auditorium, where Brianna had taken refuge in the very last row.

She was sulking. Still thinking she had blown her audition the day before. Which was stupid, because (a) twenty-four hours had passed, and (b) she had been better than 98 percent of everyone else. The problem, of course, was that she hadn't been perfect. When Brianna wasn't perfect, she suffered, and the world suffered with her.

He tried to send her a smile, but she wasn't receiving.

Her head was cocked to the left, the line of her jaw thrust forward at an angle. It reminded him of a game they used to play as kids. Six years old, maybe. Kiss Practice. Brianna would hold her head the same way, looking down and away, and Harrison would have to kiss her. Then she would rate him.

He wondered if she remembered. It wasn't the kind of thing they talked about.

"How was I?" asked Reese excitedly as she scurried into the aisle in front of Harrison.

Harrison showed her what he had written on his sheet.

"Screw you," she said, stomping away.

"Volatile," Dashiell whispered. "The word is *volatile*."

"Devon Roper," said Devon Roper, entering through the door.

"Roper the Doper," murmured Dashiell.

"Be nice," whispered Harrison. Dashiell wasn't fond of Devon. They were polar opposites. It had started freshman year when Devon had asked Dashiell if he was high. Dashiell had responded sarcastically, "Yes, aren't all Negroes?" and things had gone downhill from there.

As Devon slunk down the side aisle, his long hair swayed in front of his face and obliterated all but the smirk. "I am always nice," Dashiell whispered back. "But I don't think I can work with him if I'm student director."

"If you're *what*?" Harrison said.

"I've asked Mr. Levin for his consideration," Dashiell replied. "I think it would be a fruitful experience. What do you think?"

Harrison grinned. He hadn't ever thought of it at all. Dashiell the techie/geek, bossing people around? Dashiell was happiest relating to equipment, not humans. But he did have a habit of diving into things. Trying and trying until he really nailed it. Whenever he put his mind to something, he excelled. Well, except maybe socially. Trying to seduce Brianna during *Godspell* rehearsals with scented candles and cheese in the projection room had been pretty lame. But still. Dashiell was innocent and energetic and smart. As student director, well, Harrison had to admit it wasn't an outrageous idea. "Sounds great. But who will—?"

"Take over in the capacity of technical supervisor?" Dashiell said. "Ripley Grier. I've been training him after school and over the weekends. He is very capable. And I have no doubt he'll be a steadier, if perhaps a bit less imaginative, successor when I graduate."

Devon was onstage now, singing "Luck Be a Lady

Tonight" from *Guys and Dolls*. His voice was soft but he had a nice tone, and he seemed comfortable and confident.

"Not too bad," Harrison remarked. "We could use him in the chorus."

"You mean, the Burger Palace Boys," Dashiell said.

"Thanks, Devon!" Harrison called out. "Callbacks are Friday after school. We'll post the list that morning."

"Dude, thanks," said Devon, slinking off the stage.

"Next—Shara Simmons?"

Already coming down the aisle was a radiant, dark-skinned girl that Harrison had noticed all year without knowing her name. She was new in Ridgeport. Her eyes were a piercing green blue and they met Harrison's with a directness that belied a modest, shy smile.

"Oh . . ." said Dashiell. He was sitting straight up in his seat, his eyes fixed on Shara.

"Don't stare," Harrison murmured. "People get nervous when you stare."

He didn't have to worry. Nervous or not, Shara sang one verse of "I'm in Love with a Wonderful Guy" from *South Pacific* with a clear Broadway voice, and then belted out the second verse in a gospel style.

She wasn't even supposed to *get* to the second verse, but no one thought to stop her.

"Oh my . . ." said Dashiell.

"Maybe you can't work with her either," Harrison remarked. "She makes you monosyllabic."

"Thank you!" Dashiell blurted out. "I mean, that was great. I didn't mean to interrupt. Or cut you off."

"We do need to move on," Harrison said. "Callbacks are Friday."

"Yes," Dashiell piped up. "And, um, very professional effort."

Shara giggled. "Thank *you!*"

"She likes you," Harrison muttered.

"She thinks I'm an imbecile," Dashiell groaned.

Casey was sliding through the aisle behind Harrison now. She leaned over and whispered, "Can we let Chip Duggan go out of turn? He has been bugging me all afternoon. He has a Debate Team meeting, and he thought he would be auditioning earlier. He's blaming us for making him late. He wants to sing now."

"Tell him it's unfair to the others," Harrison said.

"He's a debater, he'll just argue with me," Casey replied. "Besides, he's convinced all the people in front of him. I think he just wore them down."

Harrison turned and noticed that someone was sitting next to Brianna in the shadows, chatting with her. Harrison couldn't make out the face. He could clearly see Chip Duggan, though, standing by the doorway, arms folded. Chip's face was tight and impatient, and as his leg jiggled, his pink socks winked over a pair of black Converses. Grimly he pointed to his watch.

"He's a perfect Eugene," Dashiell remarked. "I mean, *I'm* a perfect Eugene, but if Mr. Levin accedes to my request and names me student director, I will be barred from performing."

"Can he sing?" Harrison asked.

"Yes," Casey said. "He's been singing 'Corner of the

Sky' and some other strange tune to me every time I go into the hallway to read the list."

Harrison looked at his watch. They were running way late. If this guy could carry a tune, he would be a front-runner for the role of Eugene, the class valedictorian and number one sight gag in *Grease*. "Tell him to come straight to callbacks," Harrison said.

"But that's not procedure!" Dashiell protested.

"It'll save us time," Harrison said. "*You* said he's perfect. I agree. Let's get rid of him till Friday."

"Yes, sir," Casey said.

As she headed back to Chip, Harrison glanced at Brianna. The person next to her was laughing, his face catching a sliver of light.

"And, Casey," Harrison said, "Devon knows he's not supposed to be in here now, and so does Brianna. Kick him out."

6

pedl2METL: *how'd i do, dramakween? hmmm? am I gonna be called back, bri?*

dramakween: devon, i would tell you but then id have to shoot you.

pedl2METL: *hahahaha*

dramakween: cant comment on auds. agnst the rules. gtg.

pedl2METL: *i'm yr zuko, hands down.*

dramakween: there are lots of good parts

pedl2METL: *i didn't try out for them. if i don't get zuko, I'm out of there.*

dramakween: oh great, you're a diva too

pedl2METL: *whoa. didnt mean to piss u off.*

dramakween: im not pissed just tired.

pedl2METL: it's only 7:00

dramakween: i know. i have about 8 hrs of hw & im trying to track down kyle.

pedl2METL: kyle? jesus?

dramakween: he skipped the audition. do u know where he is.

pedl2METL: nope. but i can give u something that will help. (w the hwork. not kyle lol.)

dramakween: something??? what kind of something

pedl2METL: a little gift. i can bring it over.

dramakween: u gotta be kidding

dramakween has signed off.

Enough, Brianna decided.

When it came to the point where Devon was trying to "help" with homework, it was time to take a break. A quick trip to Starbucks to stock up on some caffeine, which at the moment was in short supply at the Glaser house, then back to the grindstone.

As Brianna drove, she hummed a show tune. She knew hundreds of them. There was a song for every mood and every situation.

In her mind now was "It Sucks to Be Me."

She couldn't shake the memory of her audition the day before. What a total disaster. She would be lucky if they cast her for anything. And with Mr. Levin allowing *Dashiell* to be student director, that possibility was out for her too.

No lead, no position at all in the biggest show of the year—wouldn't *that* just be super-duper for the old transcript. Now if she tanked on the SATs, she would really hit the trifecta.

She parked in the lot by the mall and jogged to the Starbucks. At the rate she was consuming coffee—along with her mom, the original java addict—three pounds would be about right. One Gold Coast blend, one hazelnut, one espresso. And a latte to go, for her efforts.

"Off the fingertips!" a voice shouted to her right.

Thump.

Pete Newman. Running after a football.

Farther away another voice called out, "Yo, idiot, that's my car!"

To Brianna's left, an angry middle-aged guy hustled toward the car, loaded down with shopping bags and eyeing the football smudge on his hood. Just beyond him was a sheepish-looking Kyle Taggart. "Sorry, dude," Kyle called out, "my fault!"

"Good thing that wasn't an umbrella pole," Brianna remarked.

"Oh, crap, you didn't see me do that, Brianna," Kyle said. "Yo, where you going?"

"Starbucks," Brianna replied, heading for the entrance. "I'm taking a latte break."

Kyle jogged after her and held open the door. "Yeah? They take a latte time and cost a latte money."

"I didn't hear that."

"Later, dude!" called Pete.

"That's my dad," Kyle said.

"I thought it was Pete," Brianna said.

"No! The saying. 'Latte time'? My dad says it. I didn't make it up."

Brianna grabbed the bags of coffee off the shelves and took her place in a long line. "How's Arthur?" she asked.

"Huh? Oh. Fine." Kyle nodded and shuffled his feet. "Hey, Brianna? Sorry about that night at the beach. I felt stupid. I was an ass."

"An ass, a back, legs, arms—you were all of those things. And more."

"Uh, yeah," Kyle said, reddening. "Sorry . . ."

Brianna laughed. "We missed you, Kyle. At the audition. We're going to have a tough time picking a Danny Zuko."

"Danny who?"

"Zuko. The lead role in *Grease*? You're perfect for it, Kyle. I told you that."

"Right. Yeah. I remember that. Cool."

Brianna nodded. "Okay, look. Maybe you're expecting to come straight to callbacks?"

"Uh . . ."

"Normally you can't just do that. Everyone has to go through the first round of auditions. But we'll say you didn't know, which is true, and Mr. Levin will probably make an exception—"

"Wait, whoa," Kyle said. "I wasn't even thinking about that. I can't do the show anyway. I have practice."

Brianna was not expecting that. "I thought football season was over!"

"Track."

"Next, please?" called the barista behind the counter.

"*Track?* Your ankle is *that* good?" Brianna said. "Uh, venti double latte with two percent."

"Same for me, whatever," Kyle ordered. "I'm not sprinting or anything. Just trying out for javelin. They don't have anybody for that event."

Brianna closed her eyes. Javelin. She should have known. "Kind of like a beach umbrella?" she guessed.

"That's where I got the idea."

"So it's my fault." Sighing, Brianna took her latte from the barista. "And this is okay with you—giving up the chance of a lifetime? You're an amazing actor and singer, Kyle! Didn't you hear the crowd cheer after *Godspell*? Didn't that . . . *do* something for you?"

Kyle paid for his coffee and stuffed the change in the tip cup. "It was cool. I liked it. But people cheer at track meets and football games, too."

"It's *different*—"

"Well, if *you* couldn't do drama—for whatever reason— and if you joined like the track team for a semester? And you set the record for something, like pole vault? And then, like, you *could* do drama again—but your track friends told you that you were the greatest pole vaulter ever? Which would you do?"

"The show!" Brianna said, scanning the shop. There were no empty tables and only one stool. "And I get your point. But can't you at least think it over? I have to tell you the truth, Kyle. You're letting us down. Me, Harrison, Charles, Reese, Dashiell, the Charlettes—the whole school. Think about it. What's more important, your place in the history of the Ridgeport Drama Club . . . using your talent for the good of the group . . . bringing joy to hundreds of people who will give you a standing O and never forget your performance as long as they live? Or throwing a stick?"

"Hey, come on, Brianna. There'll be more plays." He touched her gently on the arm. "I'll try out again, I promise."

His brow was scrunched with concern. All she wanted to do was hug him. And then smack him.

"Let's get out of here." She turned toward the door, singing "It Sucks to Be Me."

"Is that from a show?" Kyle asked, rushing ahead to hold the door open.

"*Avenue Q*," Brianna said.

"The one with the puppets?"

Brianna nodded as she and Kyle walked toward their cars. "It must be nice to be a puppet," she said. "It's kind of like being a human. Every once in a while someone reaches right up into your guts and twists you all around— but at least when you're a puppet, you still manage to keep your sense of humor."

"I think this means you're not happy," Kyle said.

"I had a bad audition yesterday. Totally sucked. Plus a bunch of other things. Otherwise I feel just groovy."

As she stopped before her car, Kyle gave her a tentative smile, his free hand jammed into his pocket. "Maybe you didn't do as bad as you think. You should call somebody and ask. Harrison, maybe. He'll tell you the truth."

"Yeah." She fished her keys out of her pocket. "That's not a bad idea, Kyle."

"I'm not as stupid as I look," Kyle replied.

"Hug, at least?" she said. "A prize for the loser?"

Kyle held out his cup and reached out to her awkwardly. "This," he said with a goofy smile, "could be a latte mess."

Brianna gave him a squeeze. It felt good. "I hate you," she said. "But I'm sure you'll be the best javelin thrower in the history of Ridgeport. You could always tell sucky jokes to your opponents. Psychological warfare."

Smiling, Kyle released her and bounded away toward his car.

Brianna's hands were shaking as she pulled her keys from her pocket.

7

SHE DID NOT LOOK GOOD.

Whenever Brianna came into Kostas Korner alone, she needed to talk.

Now Harrison was really concerned. Her audition had been two days ago. It was time to let go and stop obsessing. But Brianna was in one of her phases.

He had to get her out of herself.

Harrison tapped the shoulder of Niko, the waiter, as he headed to her table. "Hold on. I'm going to pretend to be her waiter, okay?"

Niko was a man of few words. He used none of them.

"It's her birthday," Harrison lied.

Niko nodded, the crags in his face twisting into a pained expression that Harrison recognized as his smile.

As Niko turned back to the kitchen, Harrison sidled up to Brianna's table. "Hello, my name is Harrison and I'll be your sex slave tonight."

"Don't tempt me," Brianna mumbled.

"Would you like to order me around? Would you like to order a half-caf, half-decaf cappuccino with fat-free half-and-half, Equal, and extra froth but no cinnamon, like someone else did tonight? If you do, you can see me split the table in half with my bare hands."

A smile. That was encouraging. "I'm in the mood for something totally self-destructive," Brianna said. "Do you have a Loser Special?"

"Um, that would be the Kostas Kitchen Sink," Harrison said. "Thirty scoops of premium third-rate-factory ice cream smothered in mostly artificial butterscotch, fudge, and strawberry sauces, all topped with canned whipped dairy product and two cancer-causing maraschino cherries."

"DON'T TELL ME HE CHANGE PRICE!" Mr. Michaels's voice boomed out. "NEXT TIME YOU TELL HIM IF HE WANTS TO RAISE PRICE, HE HAS TO TALK TO THE BOSS. ME! KOSTA!"

"Uh-oh," Brianna murmured.

"Dad's on the warpath," Harrison said, "ever since Taki the Ancient Manager retired. He expects poor Guillermo to do everything exactly the same way."

"Taki was here a thousand years," Brianna said.

"Taki and Plato?" Harrison said. "Best buds."

"HARALAMBOS!" Mr. Michaels bellowed.

"Coming," Harrison said.

Guillermo was standing by a busboy station, trying to

hold on to his dignity. He was a thin, athletic-looking guy, maybe thirty years old. His hair was jet-black and lightly moussed, and he had a quick, ready smile. He was nice to the customers and had a sense of humor, which brought a younger crowd to the diner. A breath of fresh air after Taki's sour face, threadbare white shirts, and polyester pants.

"Tell him, Haralambos," Mr. Michaels said as Harrison approached. "What Taki did when Islandwide Food Supply give to us the bill. What Taki did?"

"Taki said . . . " Harrison switched to his instant imitation of Taki. "'I don't pay until I geev beel to Onkle Kosta. No Kosta, no checkie.'"

"You see? *You see?*" Mr. Michaels said to Guillermo.

"I will not make that mistake again," Guillermo replied.

With a self-satisfied smile, Mr. Michaels turned away.

"'No checkie'?" Guillermo whispered, barely keeping a straight face.

Harrison shrugged. "I do voices. He's used to it."

"You should be respectful of your father," Guillermo replied, but without much conviction.

"Excuse me." Harrison ran over toward Brianna, just as Niko brought her a hefty grilled-cheese sandwich and a huge mug of coffee, which she barely noticed. She was doing math homework.

Harrison sat across from her. "Boo."

"I am sick," she replied.

Harrison nodded sympathetically. "We get that complaint with our coffee a lot."

"Sick about the *show*," Brianna said. "We lost our

first-choice Danny Zuko. I just talked to Kyle. He won't audition."

"Why? Is he going out for the Naked Olympics winter swim team?" Harrison asked.

Brianna lifted her head from her homework to glare at him. "Who told you about that? Reese?"

"Hey, it was a joke, okay?"

"What else did she tell you?"

"Nothing. Relax. Look, Kyle was a good Jesus, but that doesn't mean he's the best Danny." He slouched in his chair, letting his eyes sink to half-mast. "Yo, maybe youse wuzzint there, but ay, Harrison's audition? It rocked, babycakes."

Brianna rolled her eyes. "Oh God, Harrison. We all know you're an incredible actor. Many years from now, when the rest of us are fat and boring, we'll be watching you on the Oscars. Our kids won't believe we knew you. But no offense, you're no Danny Zuko. You come across smart. Intense. Danny is a big lug."

"I have outstanding lug potential. I've been working on it," Harrison said. "Look, we meet Thursday evening to decide callbacks—jeez, that's tomorrow already. If I get one, will you work with me afterward? I can do this, I know it. I never used to like the show, but I'm up for the challenge."

Brianna thought a moment, then said, "Mom and Dad are having a big dinner tomorrow night. If you come over after the meeting, we can work on it in the basement."

"And do radio shows and make fart bombs like we used to?"

Brianna broke out laughing. "Harrison, you are a class act."

"HARALAMBOS!"

Mr. Michaels, red-faced, stormed up behind him. "Hello, Brianna. Haralambos, what you doing sitting down? You see the kostomers—look! Look!" He pointed through the window at a young mom and dad with three small children, heading for a minivan in the parking lot. "They come in, look around, and leave. Why? *Because nobody serve them!*"

"Maybe they didn't like the menu," Harrison suggested.

"*Vre* Haralambos," his father said, using the unique Greek word—*vre*—that could mean anything from "jackass" to "oy vey," depending on the tone of voice. "They *love* menu—*everybody* love menu. They go 'way because nobody standing to greet them. Because you here and Niko and Guillermo in kitchen making big—"

"HAPPY BIRTHDAY TO YOU . . . HAPPY BIRTHDAY TO YOU!"

Out of the kitchen marched Niko, Guillermo, and the other two waiters, all singing out of tune and smiling at Brianna and carrying a miniature chocolate birthday cake.

"What the—?" Brianna said.

Harrison slumped down, burying his head in his hands.

8

"WAIT. START THE SCENE OVER AGAIN," BRIANNA said. She flicked on the light switch and reached out to take the script from Harrison.

He had gotten his callback, and so had Brianna. Nearly two hours ago, they had decided on the list. One thing about the Drama Club, Mr. Levin made sure decisions were fair. Drama Club officers had to leave the room during discussion, and the others would treat them exactly as they had treated everyone else who had auditioned.

Brianna's mood had lifted as soon as she found out that she made callbacks, and now Harrison was holding her to her offer—she had to coach him. On a night when she had piles of homework. Plus her mom was having a formal dinner with clients, old friends of hers from college.

But a deal was a deal.

The Glasers' basement had been reconstructed two years ago to include a small, raised stage with a separate lighting system. Facing the stage was the "house," a collection of small sofas and soft chairs. This minitheater had been a Christmas present to Brianna, one of the advantages of having a mom whose hedge-fund job brought in serious Christmas bonuses.

"Frankly, I thought that was flawless," Harrison said. He had just run through the opening scene, with Brianna reading the other parts. His hair was slicked back and he wore a tight white T-shirt and baggy, rolled-up jeans.

Upstairs, the music had been turned up in the living room. The dinner had passed the entrée phase and was headed for dessert. Which meant the end of Forced Laughter Over Highly Unfunny Stories and straight to Let's Listen to Eighties Rock and Feel Young Again. The strains of a cheesy Heart song filtered down, to great jubilant whoops of recognition. Dessert, Brianna knew, would be deeply, expensively chocolate, and mostly ignored. She could just imagine her adorably obese five-year-old brother, Colter, looking down from the bedroom stairs, drooling.

"*Almost* flawless," Brianna said. "Your walk? It's a Harrison walk. Kind of a glide. You should bounce. Like you're a boxer. Defensive. Like you're thinking, *Somebody might sneak up behind me and hit me over the head with a tailpipe.* Like if you needed to, you could turn and pop someone."

Brianna stood up and did her best fifties-tough-guy

imitation—angular body movements, awkward arms, bouncing on the balls of her feet. "Now, when ya tawk, don't go so heavy on the accent. Just act like you've got Novocain on your lower lip. Pronounce everything so you're understood, but slow it down, like talking involves too much *thinkin'*."

"Yuh, ah know what choo mean," Harrison said, bouncing on the balls of his feet. "Thank yuh vurry much, ladies 'n gennuhmun . . ."

"And cut the Elvis crap, these are working-class high school kids, okay?" Brianna glanced at the clock: 10:13. "Harrison, we went overtime. Sorry. Coaching session is over. I have to get back to homework."

"YEAAHHH!" came a voice from upstairs.

The floor began thumping. They were blasting Mr. Mister. "Kyrie Eleison." Top 40, circa 1986. To do homework in this musically toxic environment, Brianna would have to plug into her iPod and crank it up with something tolerable.

"You said till ten-fifteen!" Harrison protested. "Just one more time on the opening number, 'Summer Nights,' okay?"

"Just once," Brianna replied, plopping down into a sofa.

He began to wail, using a broomstick as a mike. He had one foot on the bar stool, the other on the bar. And he *was* good. She had to admit.

As he finished, a burst of applause came from the top of the basement stairs. Spinning around, Brianna saw her mom and about eight of her friends peering through the open door.

"*So* cute," said Mrs. Glaser. "Harrison, you are *so* cute."

"Didn't recognize him," said Brianna's dad. "Looked down here and thought, *Damn, Elvis is alive!*"

"Wull, thankyuhvurrymuch," said Harrison.

"No no no no, not *Elvis*," said Brianna.

"Can we get you any food?" Mrs. Glaser piped up. "There's lots of untouched tiramisu left over."

"*Ewwww, this is yucky!*" came Colter's voice from the kitchen.

"That doesn't mean you can throw it on the floor!" Siobhan, Colter's nanny, scolded.

"Scratch that idea," Brianna mumbled.

"I'm not hungry, but thanks," Harrison said.

The party vanished back into the kitchen, where Colter was making dramatic spitting noises.

Harrison ripped a fistful of paper towels from a rack behind the bar and began rubbing the thick gel from his hair. "Thanks, Bri. You helped a lot. Was I a lug?"

"You're better. Now go home and practice. You have till Monday."

"That's it?" Harrison grinned. "Not the most spectacular improvement ever? Not the definitive Danny Zuko of our time?"

"Next Christmas, instead of a card, I will get you a normal ego."

He grabbed the broomstick again. "From New York, live! It's the Greek radio show! With Haralambos and Briannalambos! Brought to you by . . ."

Brianna groaned. It was the fake show they used to do

in Harrison's basement when they were kids. And it was her cue. "Jen and Berry's tobacco-flavor ice cream," she said reluctantly.

"With crushed olives on top, available at Kostas Korner!" Harrison announced. "Remember Dad would run downstairs and get all mad at us and shut off the tape recorder . . ."

"He took it personally," Brianna said.

"God, yeah. That time he took out the cassette tape and actually stepped on it in his bare feet?" Harrison winced. "Blood all over the place. He acted like it was my fault. And then he bought me a football."

"To cure you of girlie interests, like satire and fun."

Harrison sank into the sofa. "God, that seems so long ago. Why do I feel like crying?"

"Because you're not only brilliant and creative, but sensitive, too," Brianna replied. "Happy? Now go home!"

Impulsively Harrison grabbed her up and planted a big kiss on her lips. "Ay, Sandy babe, a little koochie koochie for a nice job done."

Brianna pushed him away. But he stayed there, being stubbornly Danny, stubbornly in character. Waiting for her to respond.

"Later, Harrison," she said.

"Later in my drawers, baby doll," he said, bouncing off the sofa with a laugh.

She smacked him, but her heart wasn't in it.

"Hey, Bri? You know what I was thinking about the other day? Remember this?" He leaned closer and puckered his lips.

"Oh Lord . . . Kiss Practice?" She had almost forgotten about that.

Harrison laughed. But he was looking at her in a funny way, and for a minute she had this feeling that this wasn't about Danny and it wasn't about kids' games.

Which didn't make sense, because Harrison was . . . *Harrison.*

Harrison was predictable. Harrison was all about odd acting exercises. Crossing borders in the Service of Art.

He leaned closer, his eyes closing, and Brianna had a moment when it all felt wrong, as if the wires in her brain had been crossed, sparking white, forming new circuits — and suddenly, against her own better judgment, her eyes were closing, too. She felt his lips, warm and urgent. Part of her expected to recoil or laugh, but it was as if Harrison had become someone else. Not Danny, not a character in a play, but as if he had shed some kind of skin and become someone new. And the newness blotted out the sounds from upstairs, the feelings of failure and anxiety. She was thinking about other things. The warmth of his hand against her back. The sweetness of his kiss. The pressure in places where entry required a user name and password — and the shock of realizing that Harrison had somehow acquired both, without her ever noticing.

9

"YOU HOOKED UP WITH *WHO*? GOD, YOU ARE A busy girl!"

"I didn't hook up with him, Charles. And it's *whom*. And don't scream so loud. Your voice carries over the phone. And my parents are trying to sleep."

"Where are you?"

"In my bedroom. Trying to do an English paper."

"Okay, so let me summarize, Brianna. After tonight's meeting, Harrison did not go home, like all the other good little DC children. Instead, he made a beeline for Hacienda Glaser, allegedly for coaching. And now you're calling me at two in the morning—which I don't mind, darling, for events such as this, although in limited doses—because you and the Greek God of Acting made the beast with two backs, in your basement, while your parents were upstairs . . . and you expect me to take this *quietly?*"

"I don't know what got into me."

"Oh. Oh, you are setting yourself up for a response that I refuse to give."

"Chaaaaarles! We didn't . . . you know. Not completely."

"Really? Alas, there goes my twinkly mood. So, how was it? And can you at least make it sound juicy?"

"I mean, one moment I was like, oh my God, what's happening? And the next I wanted to laugh, like I was kissing my brother."

"I have visions of smeared chocolate and half-digested Teddy Grahams."

"Not *Colter*. Like a brother my own age. I've known Harrison since we were in diapers. We used to play hide-and-seek and Sardines."

"Okay, so now you're playing doctor. Think of it that way."

"*Charles, can't you be serious?* Look, this is a dilemma. And you're the dilemma guy in my life. I have one guy who's a total hottie and the biggest talent on the East Coast wanting to skinny-dip with me, and, who, it turns out, doesn't mean a thing by it. And another guy whom I used to make poop and fart jokes with, the Least Likely to Hook Up With winner sixteen years in a row, who just turned my life upside down. *What is happening to me?*"

"Hormones, hon. You feel what you feel. He's a guy, you're a girl, anything can happen. Anything can unhappen. It's what makes life fragrant and tasty. Unless, of course, you're sending me a coded message about a blessed event on the way, for which I will have to build in some extra fabric to your costume . . ."

"No! I told you no! God, why do I even bother trying to confide in you?"

"Because I'm so lovable. Unfortunately my imagination runs wild after dark. So don't get me started, for I must return to sleep. Are we finished? Did I handle the dilemma well for you? Will you be sleeping easier?"

"Eventually. I think I have to pull an all-nighter. That's part of why I'm so fried. I don't know how I'm going to get everything done."

"It's simple—don't do everything."

"Easy for you to say."

"If I'm not finished at like midnight?—that's all, folks. I grab my pj's and Anne Rice novel and ho-hum, "Night-'night!' Who needs the stress? I know I can't be perfect. That's your trouble, Brianna. You think you can be perfect. And the worst part is, maybe you can."

"Perfect has nothing to do with it! Is there anything *wrong* with trying your best?"

"I think I heard that line in a Disney movie."

"I *mean* it."

"There's nothing wrong with it. Unless it makes you a shivering, quivering remnant of your former self."

"You're reading too many vampire novels."

"Oh, but they're soooo good. And so are you, sugar."

"Thanks, Charles. You're the best."

"Just leave twenty dollars under the feather boa in the costume room. Good night, doll. Sleep tight."

"Good night."

Brianna hung up and rested her face in her hands. She actually did feel better. Hormones. It was all biological.

Blinking her eyes, she looked at her screen:

STELLA!

The Intersection of Fantasy and Reality in
Tennessee Williams's *A Streetcar Named Desire*

She began to type.

"Stellls!"

The cry rises frm the streets of New oralens, half-animal bellow and hald half chidl's wail. In teh caharcters of Staanly and blanch Tennesess Wilailmas dfemaonstrtes the conflict nbetween ytwo themes:

"Oh God . . ."

This wasn't going to work. She was so tired, her hands were sleepy. Not to mention her eyes. She blinked, but the words seemed to be playing hide-and-seek on the screen. *WAKE UP.*

She got to her feet. Her room was a mess. She picked up review materials and textbooks from the floor and piled them neatly on the corner of her desk. She shoveled all her clothes into a laundry bag. She took the humidifier container into the kitchen, filled it, and turned the humidifier on. She lit a couple of scented candles she had gotten for Christmas — "Winter Spice" and "Bracing Citrus." She hooked her iPod into her Bose docking station, scrolled to her New Orleans Music playlist, and set the volume low.

Louis Armstrong. Blues. The track said "St. James Infirmary."

It wasn't helping. All she wanted to do was crawl into bed. Pj's and an Anne Rice novel sounded pretty good.

Charles would be asleep by now. She could picture his pudgy smile. With his novel open by his bedside. Visions of vampires dancing in his head. In fabulous costumes. Looking at her pillow, she could see the shape of her own head still outlined there from last night.

Ms. Myers would give her an extension if she asked for it. Other kids had done it. Maybe she would be penalized a point or two off her grade.

Brianna sat at the edge of her mattress and sank toward the sheets. Her eyes were closing as her head hit the pillow.

And a voice piped up inside her brain, scratchy and obnoxious.

Caleb Deutsch . . .

CALE-E-E-EB DEUTSCH . . .

Such a smart boy, that Caleb. He's going to give Brianna a run for her money. Did you hear? Already took the SATs freshman year and got 2390? And what will YOU say when the class GPAs are announced and his is a 96.6871 and yours is 96.6869 . . . And there's a letter in the mailbox from Yale, and it's . . .

thin.

Ohhh, but you NEEDED YOUR SLEEP! Hey, look on the bright side! Ralph's College for Losers is a good place! And what a nice scholarship they gave you! Besides, Caleb's not going to Yale anyway! He turned them down. HE'S LEANING TOWARD HARVARD—HEEEEEHEE-HAHAHAHA!"

Eyes open. Body up.

God, that was stupid. A stupid dream. Who cared about Caleb Deutsch? Caleb was a nerd. He wasn't important.

The English paper was important. It was junior year. You did not sacrifice grades for anything. Especially sleep.

What was I thinking?

Coffee.

She needed coffee, that's all.

She grabbed all the empty vessels on her desk—two empty cans of Red Bull and mugs of coffee, hot chocolate, coffee. They looked and smelled disgusting. She brought them into the kitchen and dumped them in the sink.

Not coffee. The thought of yet another cup of Gold Coast blend made her sick. And there was no more Red Bull.

There was, however, another source of caffeine.

Mom wouldn't mind. Brianna had taken advantage before.

She walked into the hallway and upstairs. Her dad's rhythmic snores cut through the thick bedroom doorway. She knocked softly and neither of them woke up. Silently she pushed the door open and tiptoed across the carpet and into their bathroom.

Closing the door behind her, she opened the medicine cabinet above her mom's sink and flipped through the vials.

She felt ridiculous. She felt like an after-school special. *Teen girl robs parents of drugs and starts tragic spiral into substance abuse. Starring Ashley Olsen.*

There.

A box of No-Doz. Totally harmless. Nontoxic. Caffeine in pill form. Same stuff as in coffee and Coke, for God's sake. Recommended dose, two pills. Equivalent to two cups of coffee.

She spilled four into her hand. No, five. Just in case it wasn't enough. She would take only the amount needed, no more. Enough for two, maybe three hours. Then they would wear off and she could get a good three hours' sleep.

Cupping them in her left hand, she ran back downstairs to the kitchen.

10

CASEY YAWNED, PROPPING HER KNEE AGAINST HER locker door. She wanted to feel that Friday rush that everyone else seemed to be feeling as they ran through the pre-homeroom hallway. But today was callbacks, which meant work. Lots of work. Making decisions, answering complaints. Arguing.

Resting her shoulder bag on her thigh, she rummaged through the bag, looking for the callback sheet. The *only* existing hand-corrected list. Not in her shoulder bag. Groaning, she peered into the open locker. Inside, the top shelf was jammed with papers and books, like a trash compacter. On the hooks hung coats from the summer, fall, and winter, at least two of each, some of which she could neither see nor recall owning. A pile of shoes rose from the floor, meeting the hems of the coats and creating a space blockage of nearly 100 percent.

Casey did not like exposing the inside of her locker for all to view. It was highly embarrassing. Everything else in her life—her room, her notes, the way she approached stage-managing—was orderly and neat. Somehow the locker was the thing that took the hit for the rest of it. And there was a good chance that she had stuffed the callback sheet in there somewhere. She couldn't remember.

"I'm starting to worry about you, Casey," said a familiar voice behind her.

"Me, too," Casey replied. "Brianna, do you have the callback sheet? Say yes, please. Or I may have to take everything out to find it."

"We'll do it together. It'll be like archaeology. Maybe we'll find the mummified remains of King Tut." Brianna quickly opened her own locker. "Me? I gave up on neatness. But my boys love me anyway. Right, boys?"

She planted a kiss on the smiling face of a photo of Adam Pascal from *Rent*. The inside of Brianna's locker door was covered with photos of Broadway stars.

"Got it!" Casey said, pulling a blue folder marked CALLBACKS from a loose-leaf binder.

"You see, it's just a matter of sticking with it," Brianna said, slamming her locker shut. "That's what Charles doesn't understand."

"Charles?" Casey asked. She shut her locker and fell into step with Brianna, heading toward the auditorium.

"He thinks sleep is the most important thing," Brianna said. "It's overrated. I Googled articles about sleep last night. Did you know you can control your tiredness? You can be wide-awake even if you didn't sleep much. You just have to know when you reach your peak REM cycle. That's the so-called Rapid Eye Movement stage of sleeping. You have only a few of them each night. Everybody's a little different, so the cycle could be two or three hours. So all you have to do is set your alarm so you wake up at the end of a cycle!"

Casey examined Brianna's face. Her eyes were bloodshot and her skin seemed a little pale. "Guess you didn't get much sleep last night, huh?"

"I finished my report on *Streetcar* at four in the morning, slept about two hours and fifteen minutes, and I'm totally rested. Totally ready for my callback." As they turned a corner, Brianna shouted out, "Stu Pimsler—where were you earlier this week? How come you didn't audition?"

A hulking, stoop-shouldered guy turned from where he was leaning against a wall. "Audition? Me?"

"We saved the lead role for you, dude. We needed someone hot and sexaaaay, and we asked, 'Where's Stu?' And you weren't there! You were off in a cloud of babes, I guess. Hey, your choice."

The left side of Stu's lip, working harder than it was used to, curled upward in a grin. "Huh-huh. Right."

"The biting wit," Brianna said to Casey. "That always kills me."

Casey stifled a laugh. When Brianna was in a mood, she did this kind of thing. Tossed off outrageous comments to any and everyone. Casey knew the comments were engineered, more than anything else, to make *her* blush. It was a game Brianna always got right. The little jabs never seemed to hurt—somehow the person would always take them just the right way. "Someday you're going to regret saying stuff like that," Casey warned.

"Like what—making Stu feel like a million dollars? I gave him something to cheer up his drab and dull afternoon. I'm like a social worker. They should pay me."

At the auditorium, a crowd was gathering. Casey posted the callback list on the auditorium door and quickly ducked away.

Instantly the crowd converged, shoving and shouting. Cries of "yes!" and "all riiiight!" mixed with an occasional "aw, crap," "I can't believe this," and outright sobbing.

"Let's get out of here," Brianna said, "before they kill us."

Casey ran to her locker after last class. "Are we ready?" she said excitedly.

Brianna was staring into a compact mirror, putting on blush, and warming up her voice. "Ee-ohhh, ee-ohhh, ee-ohhh . . . " she sang. "Reddeee, reddeee, I ammmm reddeeeee . . . "

"Let's go!" Casey took Brianna's arm and they both raced downstairs.

Outside the auditorium, kids were helping one another put on makeup and adjust clothing so that it looked convincingly fiftieslike. Casey blinked at the size of the crowd. There were too many people. Faces who didn't belong there. People who had definitely been cut after the first audition.

Casey checked her clipboard.

"Hiiiii, Casey!" shouted a girl who hadn't even made it through four bars of her audition song. "I was wondering if I could sing again? Because Tuesday I had like the worst strep throat ever."

A guy with a thatched hut of hair and a knobby Adam's apple nodded furiously. "Me, too. So like, if you had like, some time after everybody else?"

Casey backed away as questions flew from all sides:

"When they said, 'Thank you,' didn't that mean you were automatically called back?"

"Phil? He's number thirteen? He can't do the show and told me I could take his place."

"My name wasn't on the callback sheet—Bill Federman? But I think you *meant* to call me back? I was the guy who sang 'Sit Down, You're Rocking the Boat' . . . and you were all laughing and smiling . . . ?"

"It's just that I played Frenchy in summer camp and I know I could do it better than anybody . . . "

"Um, well . . . " Casey said. "I don't know, I guess we could ask . . . "

Brianna grabbed her arm. "What are you *saying*, Casey? This isn't a free-for-all. You can't do that. If you let one of them change your mind, they'll all cry unfair."

She was right. Casey nodded. "Um, listen. People? If your name isn't on the callback sheet, sorry, but—"

"But could I talk to Mr. Levin?" interrupted a guy with a wispy beard.

"I was sick Monday and Tuesday—"

"Who's in charge?"

"Brianna? *Brianna?* You were the one who said I should try out! Why did you cut me?"

"*Will you all just shut up!*" Brianna wheeled on Casey. "*You're* the stage manager, Casey. Stage-manage!"

Casey recoiled. "Brianna?"

Brianna's face fell. "Sorry. I—I'm like on another planet today. Don't take anything I say seriously. I love you, Case. I'll see you in a minute. But I have to prepare an audition."

Casey swallowed hard as Brianna ran across the hall and disappeared into the bathroom.

"Next callback, number eleven, Harrison Michaels!" Dashiell called out.

Brianna watched as Harrison jumped on the stage, whipping out his comb and spitting on it before running it through his hair, which had been styled and greased to within an inch of its life.

And he was *bouncing*. On the balls of his feet. Just like she had coached him.

The day had been rough, especially during the last two periods, when her lack of sleep had kicked in. She had slept through history. If it hadn't been for the little caffeine pill she had tucked away, she might not be awake now. Bringing it had been a stroke of genius. So much more convenient than coffee. And kinder to your breath. *Not to mention safe and non-habit-forming. Says so right on the box! Complete with exclamation point!*

Now, seeing Harrison, she felt alert again.

"Yeah, well, I'm gonna sing," Harrison announced,

"and if anybody gives me gas, yer outta here." He turned upstage and tripped over a music stand, stumbled to the floor, and then made a big production out of getting to his feet and trying to put the stand aright. "Hey. Sorry," he said, then pointed to Ms. Gunderson. "Uh, my note, Monstro?"

Slapstick. Danny needed to be good at slapstick. They hadn't worked on that, really. But he knew. Harrison's instincts were perfect.

Ms. Gunderson, her shoulders shaking from laughter, played an E flat.

Harrison swung into "I'm All Shook Up." His fifties hip movements, his air guitar, his sneer—they were amazing. Not a false move.

Brianna felt herself beaming. She hadn't allowed herself to think about what had happened the night before. She and Harrison hadn't really talked about it. He had left in a hurry, when her parents had called downstairs. And all that day she had hidden the whole incident in a dark corner at the back of her mind, blocking it out in the stress of the callbacks.

Part of her knew this would happen—she wouldn't think about Harrison until she had to. At his audition. Part of her had hoped that when she looked back at the night before, she would realize it was nothing. Something to laugh about. Another Brianna–Harrison memory, like the radio shows.

But it wasn't that. Not at all. Harrison had changed. Or maybe she had.

He had to feel the same way. Something like that was

too big to forget. As he finished to a round of applause, she wanted to run up onstage and hug him. "Woo-HOOOO!" she shouted, throwing him a double thumbs-up.

"Da-a-a-a-nny!" Reese screamed in a swoon.

Harrison glanced across the audience. His eyes briefly swept past Brianna and locked on Reese. He threw her a wink and a kiss and swaggered offstage.

"Nice job," Brianna said, but he was gone.

He was acting, she said to herself, glancing at Reese.

The rest of the afternoon was a haze of listening and scrawling comments on the evaluation sheets. Just before it was Brianna's turn, she raced to the back of the house and quickly did her breathing exercises.

"Brianna Glaser, take it away!" Dashiell called out.

Brianna bounded down the aisle. "Break a leg, dollface!" Charles whispered as she passed.

"Thanks!" she replied in her best Sandy voice.

She smiled at everyone. She threw a big one to Harrison in the second row. He was looking at his eval sheet, not at her. Which was fine. Appropriate. Professional.

Brianna hit her mark center stage. Feeling the heat of the spotlight, she smiled.

Peter Mansfield played the intro to Brianna's favorite *Grease* song. The "Look at Me, I'm Sandra Dee" reprise. The transformation number at the end of the show, where Sandy stops being a wimp and takes Rizzo's advice—if you really want to get the man, be trashy! It was the moral of the whole show.

She hit the first note on the button.

Yes.

As the notes left her mouth they sailed over the seats.

Yes, *YES.*

It was all there. Movement, voice, character.

It was *working*!

At the end of the number Brianna dramatically stuffed tissues in her bra, struck a pose, and ended with a belt that would have made Jennifer Hudson proud. Charles jumped out of his seat cheering, until a sharp "be professional" look from Harrison stopped him cold.

What was *that* all about?

Casey hopped onto the stage with two scripts. "Now for the line readings. Um, how about Act One, Scene Six, where Sandy and Danny finally meet away from the other kids? Who wants to read Danny—Harrison?"

Harrison looked startled. "Uh, sure."

He walked toward the stage, a sheepish smile on his face.

Sheepish. That was something. Harrison wasn't usually sheepish. He definitely had some thoughts about last night.

Stay in character, Brianna told herself. She smiled brightly back.

"Let's start here," Harrison said, pointing into his script.

He had written something on a yellow Post-it note, and he held the script so no one else could see.

I'm a jerk. Sorry.

Brianna nodded. But that was not what she expected. *A jerk* for kissing her? What was last night all about?

What exactly was he sorry for?

Use it, Brianna. Use the emotions for the scene.

She tore into a Rydell cheer, shaking imaginary pompoms. Harrison broke in, as Danny. Apologizing. He and Sandy had met over the summer. Sandy was a new kid, so he didn't even realize they were in the same school. She thought he had another girlfriend, etc., etc. The scene was painful. Tense. Perfect.

And Brianna realized the method to Harrison's madness. His note had had a purpose. It was setting the emotional core of the scene. Of course.

Thank you, Harrison.

When it was over, Dashiell stood up. He was wearing a very un-Dashiell corduroy sport jacket and baseball cap. His director's uniform. "Thank you," he said in a formal voice. "We will make our final decisions over the weekend. As you know, of course."

"Thanks!" Brianna waved to everybody in an enthusiastic Sandy-like way. "Go ahead and call the next person. I'm going to catch my breath in the back of the auditorium."

She jogged toward the rear, taking deep breaths. Getting the heart rate down. Harrison had slunk into his seat without a word to her.

She had nailed the part. She just *knew* it. Everything that went wrong about the initial audition had just gone right. Her only competition so far was Reese. But Reese was the wrong type for Sandy. Too bold and sexy. Reese was more of a Rizzo type, the tough girl.

"Nice audition, Brianna," Casey whispered, standing by the auditorium door.

Brianna smiled. "Thanks," she said.

"Are you feeling okay?"

"Great!" She put her arm around Casey. Casey was the bomb. "Hey, you're doing a great job. I'm *so* sorry I snapped at you before."

"If I were auditioning, I would have been stressed, too," Casey replied. "No worries. Okay, next—Chip? Chip Duggan?"

Brianna found her clipboard and sat down. Harrison, Dashiell, and Reese had their backs to her, but Charles couldn't help turning to her and twinkling as only he could.

As Chip walked to the stage, Brianna doodled on a spare sheet:

Sandy Dumbrowski.........................Brianna Glaser
Brianna Glaser enjoys gardening and Havana cigars, but only after midnight. She gives a big wooohoooooooo to her peeps in the DC who have taught her everything she knows about bobby soxxs, hot rod waxing, and yak-herding. COLTER, I LOVE YOU! XXXXXOOOO

"Johnny O'Co-o-o-onnor bought an automobiiiile . . ."

Chip was singing, his body contorted into some weird position as if he were trying to pray but had to go to the bathroom. It was a weird song, something about a guy, his girlfriend, and a car that kept breaking down.

"Thanks, Chip," Dashiell called out about halfway through the number. "Where did you get that song?"

"It's a signature song of the Harvard Krokodiloes," Chip said, "of whom I hope someday to become a member."

"It's not really a fifties song," Dashiell remarked. "We asked for a fifties song."

"Agreed," Chip replied. "Point well taken. It actually comes from the twenties—but in its way, it conveys the concerns of guys in the fifties. Cars, girls, problems connecting socially. And it amused me more than the doo-wop songs of the period, which don't really show off the voice without a doo-wop chorus."

Strange song, eh voice, good debater, Brianna wrote on her eval sheet.

Casey walked onstage, handing Chip a script. "Here are the sides for the character Eugene. Your lines are highlighted in yellow. I'll read all the other parts."

"I'm n-not familiar with the p-part," Chip said, suddenly seeming nervous, "but I—I'll give it a girl . . . a *whirl*."

Brianna looked up.

Could it be . . . ?

Casey, watch out . . . she wrote.

In Casey's presence, Chip was paralyzed. Nervous, awkward, overeager. Having him read for the character Eugene the nerd was perfect.

When he was done, he insisted on reading further. He tried to argue that he hadn't "demonstrated the full range of his abilities."

"Probably true. But we have to continue," Dashiell insisted. "We have all the info upon which to base an evaluation."

"Shara Simmons?" Casey called out as Chip skulked offstage.

"Here!" chirped Shara, skipping down the aisle.

Dashiell leaped up from his seat and walked up the aisle to greet her. He was grinning from ear to ear. "Thank you for coming, Shara. It will be great to hear you again."

Casey, who had taken a seat next to Brianna, gave Brianna a knowing look. "Love is in the air," Brianna said.

But her eyes were on Shara.

She had pulled her hair into a ponytail, which was bobbing up and down as she ran toward the stage. She was wearing bobby socks and a white knit cardigan sweater with a familiar varsity letter *R* sewn on. "Go, Rydell!" she squealed.

The Ridgeport *R* very conveniently stood in for Rydell, the fictional high school in *Grease*.

Smart. Very smart. Brianna wished she had thought of it.

As Shara sang, Brianna sank deeper into her seat. Shara was good. She had that kind of innocence needed for the part. A little stiff, maybe. Not as polished as she could be. But she could really give Brianna a run for her money.

Brianna scribbled on her eval sheet:

Excellent voice . . . but acting?

Harrison was taking notes furiously.

"Thank you, Shara. Can you read for us, please?" Casey said, walking toward the stage with sides for the role of Sandy. "Can we get a volunteer to read for Rizzo?"

Dashiell leaped up like a puppy. "I'll read!"

"Rizzo is a girl," Brianna reminded him. "Let me."

She set down her clipboard and walked toward the stage.

Rizzo was easy. Brianna would show Shara what it meant to *act*. She would remind Harrison who taught him to be Danny.

She smiled as she mounted the stage. Shara looked nervous.

"Don't worry," Brianna whispered. "You're very good. You'll be cast in something."

She cleared her throat and began to read.

11

"YOU *WHAT?*" BRIANNA SAID.

"We all agreed," Harrison said. "It's the best decision."

Brianna leaped up from the chair in Mr. Levin's den. His house was small, and his kids were watching *Finding Nemo* in the basement, so she could not scream, even though she wanted to.

She thought she had been prepared for the Saturday casting meeting. She knew some choices would be tough. But when the other DC officers had sent her out of the room to discuss her audition, her gut feeling had been good.

She hadn't expected this.

"What are you guys *thinking?*" she blurted out. "I'm not right for *Rizzo!*"

Just saying *I* and *Rizzo* in the same sentence was too bizarre. She had auditioned for *Sandy*. She had worked out Sandy's songs, her lines.

"You're an actor, Brianna—"

"Was Shara that much better? *Did I suck that bad?*"

"Those are two different questions."

"And the answers are yes and yes!" Brianna slammed her hands down on the windowsill with a thump, staring out into the icy afternoon. Shara was a beginner. Talented and pretty, but . . . "Was it because of Dashiell? He has such a crush on her—"

"Your audition was great, Brianna," Harrison said. "Really great. And Shara was good, too. But Shara can *only* play Sandy. She wouldn't be able to do any other part. You can act. When you read Rizzo's part—with Shara reading Sandy—well, we knew you were versatile, but you really nailed Rizzo. Everybody was blown away. Plus you and Shara looked perfect together."

"But Reese—"

"Reese is playing Frenchy. The beauty school dropout." Harrison shrugged.

Brianna nodded. She could hear the others wrapping up in Mr. Levin's living room, discussing the rehearsal schedules.

"Brianna, look, I know how you feel." Harrison was moving close, looking into her eyes. "I always want to play the hero. But I always get the character role. It's what happens when you have talent."

"And modesty," Brianna said.

"I didn't mean it that way."

"You've been doing a lot of things you don't mean to do."

Harrison took a deep breath. "Yeah. I guess . . . we should talk about that."

"Well, we've been busy."

"I tried to apologize . . ."

"Apologize for what?"

Harrison was turning red. "That night . . . I don't know what happened. I didn't mean to . . . it was a mistake."

She tried to look him in the eye, but he glanced away. "Really? Was it? I mean, it didn't feel too bad to me, Harrison."

He grimaced.

The circuits were crossing again. Nothing was making any sense.

What? What could she say to him? *I thought everything had changed.* How realistic was that?

Brianna turned and went for the door. "I think they want us," she said.

She left before he could see her cry.

RIDGEPORT DRAMA CLUB
FINAL CAST LIST

Director, Mr. Greg Levin
Student Director, Dashiell Hawkins
Musical Supervisor, Ms. Liesl Gunderson
Student Musical Director, Peter Mansfield

** First rehearsal, Tuesday, January 22 **
** First performance, Friday, March 21 **

Danny Zuko . . . . Harrison Michaels
Sandy Dumbrowski . . . . Shara Simmons
Kenickie . . . . Barry Squires
Betty Rizzo . . . . Brianna Glaser
Frenchy, Sandy's friend . . . . Reese Van Cleve
Jan . . . . Aisha Rashid
Marty . . . . Kate Luongo
Doody . . . . Ethan Smith
Roger . . . . Dino Testaverde
Sonny . . . . Corbin Smythe
Vince Fontaine . . . . Hassan Baig
Eugene Florczyk . . . . Chip Duggan
Teen Angel . . . . Sammy Wilkens
Johnny Casino . . . . Jamil Moore
Miss Lynch . . . . Jenny Koh
Cha-Cha . . . . Lynnette Freeman
Patty Simcox . . . . Deirdre O'Connor

Part 2
Greased Lightning

January 22

12

"SETTLE DOWN, EVERYONE!" DASHIELL CRIED OUT. He was buzzing about, wearing a baseball hat printed with the word DIRECTOR. Looking up to the projection booth, he shouted: "Ripley? Cue 25B!"

The houselights immediately went out, casting the auditorium in darkness as a small but bright spotlight lit Dashiell on the stage. "Welcome, thespians all! It's Tuesday, the first rehearsal for the annual Ridgeport High School spring production!"

Harrison, onstage stretching out the kinks in his hamstring, gave Charles a look.

"Do you think he's into it enough?" Charles asked.

"Give him a chance, he'll be great," Reese said. "Straighten your leg, Harrison."

"Dashiell," Mr. Levin said softly, "I think I'd prefer houselights up."

"*Ripley*? Reverse it!" Dashiell called out. "Okay, people! We will be rehearsing on Tuesdays, Wednesdays, and Fridays until Tech Week, at which point—"

As the auditorium lit up again, a familiar voice boomed from the back of the auditorium, "GOD BLESS AMERICA AND DON'T FORGET THE GREEKS!"

Harrison's back seized up in midstretch. He couldn't help it. With a yowl, he collapsed to the stage.

It was the voice.

Reese, who three nanoseconds ago had been helping him with his dance technique, was gone. Along with all the other members of the DC, she was following the sound of the voice.

All of them, racing off to greet the Pied Piper of Ridgeport, Kostas Michaels. "Kosta" or "Gus" to his friends, which seemed to include everyone.

"I think this is the *real* reason people join the Drama Club," said Shara Simmons as she walked by Harrison. "Um, do you need a hand?"

"No, I'll be fine," replied Harrison, struggling to his feet.

It was a tradition—every year since Harrison was a freshman. The first rehearsal of Spring Musical meant a catered celebratory Kostas Korner meal.

Not that Kosta actually cared about the theater. But he was well aware that the Drama Club was the center of life in Ridgeport, and anyone with a decent sense of business knew where to look for loyal customers. If there was anything his dad had, it was business sense.

"TIME TO EAT! IS KOSTA TREAT!" he intoned.

The same lines over and over. Oral tradition.

Kosta was bustling down the aisle now, winking at Harrison, winking at the pretty girls, balancing a huge cellophane-wrapped plate of sandwiches, rebuffing everyone's offers of help.

"*Help* me? Ha! You eat my food, you help me! I bring back empty trays, you help me!" Kosta spoke in exclamations.

Behind him marched Niko and two other employees with a tub of pastitsio, a baked pasta dish with a cream sauce; an enormous salad/hors d'oeuvres plate; and a heaping pile of pastries.

"*TI KANEIS, KYRIOS MICHALAKIS?*" came Dashiell's voice over the loudspeaker.

"Bravo! Is Dashiell? Dashiell speak Greek? He's make me proud!"

"THOSE ARE THE ONLY WORDS I KNOW!" Dashiell announced.

"Ho ho!" Kostas laughed. "*Vre Haralambos, éla, éla!*"

Damn it, Harrison, come on, come on!

Harrison struggled to his feet. His right hamstring was throbbing. As the trays were set down near the edge of the stage, he knelt and began carefully peeling back the cellophane.

"I know where you get it from," said Reese, picking up a stuffed grape leaf and winking at Harrison as she set it slowly on her tongue. "That animal thing. Mmm. Your dad is sexy. In an old-guy way."

Harrison picked up a slice of roast beef and ripped it in half with his teeth. "Rrrrowff."

"Reese, Reese!" Mr. Michaels bellowed, giving Reese a big hug. He turned to Harrison and winked. "Ooh la la."

With a sigh, Harrison stood up. He had to get rid of this leg cramp, not to mention the faint sense he got whenever his father did stuff like this—the inner feeling of a curdling soul. As he headed to the Green Room, he spotted Brianna in her usual place in the shadows at the rear of the auditorium. She was reading the script, gesturing and making faces. Trying different approaches to Rizzo.

He felt relieved. He had been worried about her. She could be a first-class diva. But she was also a trouper.

The Green Room still smelled of fresh paint. A gleaming metal barre ran along three sides of the room, a wall-size mirror on the other. He lifted his sore leg to the barre and massaged it.

"Flex the foot," came Reese's voice from the door.

"I thought you were eloping with Dad," Harrison said.

"Ha ha." She walked beside him, gently putting one hand on Harrison's hip and the other on his leg. "Now slowly lean forward and feel the burn. Keep the hip forward. See? Look in the mirror. It creates a better line and gives you balance."

"Thanks." The stretch stung, but he could feel the knot unraveling in his hamstring.

"Let's try a combination, to limber up." Reese rushed over to a boom box tucked into a corner and pressed the On switch.

A dance tune blared out. "If I Close My Eyes." Good song.

"Okay, ready?" Reese said. She stood in front of him, grabbing the barre, as the intro played. "Do what I do. And-a ONE-two-three-four . . ."

As she lifted her arm, he watched the small movements in her back.

Funny, he thought. You never really thought about backs. You were a breast guy or a leg guy, a butt man, whatever. You never heard anyone say, "Damn, what a back."

But there was something about a long, curved dancer's back. It was hot.

"Third position, first position, left arm up!"

Harrison followed along as best he could. He wished he had turnout like hers. His feet were lumpy and thick and pointed straight ahead. Reese's turned out.

Turned-out feet were hot, too.

Reese turned to face him. "*What* are you looking at?" she said with a curious smile.

"Nothing."

"I could see that look on your face in the mirror."

"You're supposed to be helping me," Harrison said, "not having fantasies."

"*Fantasies?* Who's the one having fantasies?"

"Wishful thinking."

Reese rolled her eyes. "Back in fourth grade again, are we? I know you, Harrison. You can't help yourself. You're more like your dad than you think. But that really bothers you. So you bury it."

"Thank you, Professor Freud. But I'm not like my dad at *all*."

"Why do you think I'm always coming on to you? Because of your hot body? Because I dream about you day and night? It's because I love watching the way you react. You *are* like your dad, but you can't allow yourself to show it. When you get turned on, it scares you. And then you try so hard to squash that feeling."

"Glad I entertain you so much," Harrison said. "So if I ripped your clothes off, you would leave me alone?"

Reese gave him a long, appraising look. "You know, Harrison," she said, "if you bury things, sooner or later they always surface. You can't hide it, dude. Like the way you look at Brianna? I'm not stupid. Something happened between you two. But it never got finished. Why don't you just make up your mind and go for it?"

Harrison nearly choked, but he turned the sound into a laugh. "You're crazy."

Reese walked up close to him. "I also know you're really not into me, but I can help you be a better dancer if you just take me seriously."

She turned away and began doing an arabesque, singing along with the tune. *"Tell me what happens, when you stop being lonely . . . "*

Through the door he could hear muffled chatting and laughing, but most of all the bluff, deep voice of Kostas Michaels.

"Let's see a demi-plié . . ." Reese said, turning around to face him.

Harrison fought the impulse to answer her back. Knock

the chip off her shoulder. But Reese was Reese. You had to take her with a grain of salt. And admire the view. He allowed himself to bend his knees, slowly sinking lower, until his eyes were at her level.

If I close my eyes [the lyrics of the song rang out] *I will still see you, right here by my side,*
Hold me close, whisper in my ear:
Everything will be all right . . .

"Good," she said, smiling. "Now relax your shoulders."

It was a nice smile.

No, it wasn't!

Yes, it was.

Her arms settled around his shoulders now. He felt something inside, but he wasn't sure what.

Was it a buried feeling, like Reese said? Did he have buried feelings? What did a buried feeling feel like? And how could she be right, anyway? He was *good* at feelings. Everyone said so. A great actor was all about feelings. Bringing them up, projecting them to an audience.

He tried to imagine what Judd, the character he played in *Oklahoma!*, would feel in this situation. Okay, bad example, Judd was a creep. John the Baptist in *Godspell*, he was cool.

The thing was, it was easy when you could hide behind a script. When someone else put words in your mouth. Real feelings sucked. They were messy. You couldn't control them. Like the other night with Brianna. He hadn't buried anything then. Maybe he *should* have.

He could smell Reese now, earthy-sweet and close.

"Keep going," she said.

He lowered himself into another plié, but his balance was off. He was tipping forward.

"Uh, Harrison?"

"Huh?" His eyes sprang open. He fell forward, toward her. She released her hand from the barre.

"Harrison, what are you doing?"

Thump.

They both hit the floor, Harrison on top. She was looking at him as if he had lost his mind. "Harrison, were you like, trying to kiss me? What the hell? I didn't mean for you to take me *that* seriously!"

"No! I wasn't! You said keep going!"

Reese burst out laughing. "You were doing a plié. You're not supposed to come forward. You're supposed to *go down! Go down!*"

At that moment the door flew open.

"OH!" came a high-pitched shriek.

Harrison and Reese untangled themselves and spun around. Charles was in the doorway, a half-eaten piece of baklava in his left hand. "Hi, kids," he said, backing out through the door. "Uh, okay, *toodles*, then. I didn't see a thing."

13

WHERE WERE HARRISON AND REESE? WHERE was Charles? Casey could not believe the disorganization. Everyone was eating. Three DC officers had disappeared. And now Dashiell, Mr. Levin, and Ms. Gunderson were getting antsy about starting.

She raced onto the stage, passing Chip in the left aisle.

"Should I put a sock in my pants?" he asked.

Casey wasn't sure she heard right. "Sorry, say that again?"

"I heard a documentary on NPR about the fifties, David Halberstam or somebody," Chip replied. He was dressed in a white T-shirt and extremely tight jeans that made his legs look like sticks. He had a fake tattoo, but his arm was so skinny Casey couldn't discern the image—either a naked girl or a car. "Apparently guys would routinely put a sock in their pants to attract women. Sort of like a peacock's plumage?"

"Peacock?"

Chip's face quickly reddened. "So to speak."

Casey looked over his getup. He looked like a greaser. Like Danny Zuko. Eugene was not supposed to look like Danny Zuko. Eugene was supposed to wear tattersal shirts, creased blue khaki pants, penny loafers. "Chip, have you read the script yet?" she asked.

"Just a summary online. Saturday was the big CFL tournament—Catholic Forensics League, that is—and I had to prepare an opinion on the legacy of the Ottoman Empire in the possible reconstruction of the Middle East—"

"Okay, well, anyway, we're going to start at the top— Act One, Scene One, and you're in it—so don't worry about costuming right now, okay?" Casey said, heading backstage. "Is there anyone in the Green Room?"

Charles was rushing across the backstage area. "Reese and Harrison," he said. "Um, but you *may* not want to go in there just yet . . ."

"What are they doing?" Casey said.

Beep Beep! The sound made Casey jump. Vijay Rajput, one of the Charlettes, raced by carrying an old-fashioned car horn. "Excuse me!" he shouted.

"Excuse us!" shouted some other Charlettes, Gabe Hirsch and Ashley Mangione, who were carrying a tailpipe, two hubcaps, windshield wipers, and a wooden box, all balanced precariously between them.

"What are *those?*" Charles demanded.

"Car parts," Gabe said. "For *Greased Lightning.* The hot rod. My dad says we can have it all. He runs the salvage yard? There's more outside, in the pickup."

"We're building a fake car, not a real one!" Charles replied, holding his forehead.

"Don't be so *verklempt,*" Vijay said. "It's just a play."

"Ladies and gentlemen? Can we start?" Dashiell called out.

Casey tentatively approached the Green Room. Before she could knock on the door, Harrison and Reese barged out. They immediately split and sat at opposite sides of the auditorium.

Casey gave Charles a look. He lifted his eyebrows and started whistling softly.

What was going on here? There were rumors about Brianna and Kyle, Brianna and Harrison—and now Harrison and Reese?

The cast members were sitting in the auditorium, chattering and gorging on the food. Brianna was in the back, doing homework.

Dashiell flung his scarf around his neck with a flourish. "Now let's put away the comestibles, gather up front, and have a read-around. Top of the play. Flash forward to the future, Rydell High Class of '59 homecoming. Let's skip the song and go to the speaker, Eugene." Dashiell read from the script. "Eugene was the class valedictorian. Unlike the others, he's uncoordinated and has a squeaky voice. He's overconfident and pompous, but easily fooled."

Chip's face fell. "Wait. Can I read that description?"

Mr. Levin handed him a script, explaining, "Eugene is the comic foil. The kind adults love but other kids like to hate. And he opens the show as the speaker at the reunion."

"Foil?" Chip said. He frowned, then began reading the speech in a subdued voice.

Casey quickly got the scripts to everyone and sat. It was a great cast, but part of her wished Devon Roper had agreed to play the part they had given him. He would have been a perfect greaser, but he only wanted to play Danny.

Ah well.

The bad thing about read-arounds, Casey had learned, was that they always sucked. It was hard to read a play cold. The good thing was that you could only go up from there.

Sort of. Everyone seemed to pick up steam except Brianna. Her readings of Rizzo were flat and lifeless.

At the first break, Casey caught Brianna in the lobby. "Is everything all right?" she asked. "You seem upset."

"Fine," Brianna said.

"You're not mad, are you?" Casey said. "About being cast as Rizzo?"

"Nope. I like a challenge. I'm just marking, that's all. Just for this reading. I want to hear the lines before I start to get into them dramatically."

"So . . . you're angry at Harrison?"

"I see *everyone's* talking about my personal life," Brianna snapped.

"Brianna, hey, come on, you can talk to me. I'm your best friend."

"I don't know, Casey. I'm just trying to keep my head above water. I don't know what Harrison wants from me. I don't know what Kyle wants. I don't know what I want. The thing is, none of that really matters. The show matters. But thanks for asking."

With that, she headed back into the auditorium.

Casey felt a headache coming on.

By the end of the read-around, only the faculty advisers seemed happy. And Dashiell. "That was remarkable, vivid yet understandably inchoate," he said. "Now let's take five and then tackle the opening production number."

As Ms. Gunderson went to the piano, Casey huddled with Dashiell, who had started marking up the script with notes. "How am I doing?" he asked eagerly.

"I understand about *half* of what you're saying," Casey replied. "But I think you're doing great."

"I wish I could say the same about Ripley." Dashiell's reggae ringtone sounded from his pocket. "He appears to have self-esteem issues. He calls every ten seconds. Excuse me."

Casey glanced toward the stage. Chip Duggan was walking briskly up the aisle, his face glum. "Casey, I don't think I can do this role," he said. "I'm not feeling the character."

"We just started, Chip—"

"I don't know if I'm up to the acting challenge. Eugene is a comic tour de force and I'm not a comic guy. I would have to study to learn how to be funny. I thought I was going to be a greaser."

Casey sighed. Stage-managing was hard. You had to do so many things that were not in the job description. "Chip," she said softly. "You *get* it. You get the humor without even trying. You are a natural. You saw Kyle in *Godspell*, right? Same thing. Like Kyle, when you step on the stage, you inhabit the character."

"But I'm nothing like Kyle—"

"In terms of what you give the audience, you are. You will get tons of applause. Do you really want to rob them of that chance?"

"That's a creative spin, Casey, and I appreciate the effort."

"It's not a *spin*. Chip, you have to stop overthinking these things—"

"You don't know what it feels like to be laughed at," Chip snapped. His eyes were suddenly red. "I like acting, okay? I like being someone else. If you were me, would you *want* to be Eugene—more of the same, only worse—so people can laugh even more?"

"That's exactly how you work it through!" Casey said. She caught her breath, thinking about Westfield, Connecticut, about the idiot kids in her elementary school who would pull on the sides of their eyes to be "Chinese." "I know something about stereotypes, Chip. If you try to ignore or deny or hide, people will nail you. If you play into the image—if you own it—the problem goes away. You can confront it, you can do it with humor. If you let them *know* you know, you take away their ammunition."

"I hadn't thought of it that way . . ." Chip said, sounding surprised. "Casey, have you thought of joining the debate team?"

Casey grinned. "If you play Eugene, I'll agree to . . . think about it!"

Chip looked over his shoulder, sighed, and straightened himself up. "I'll give it a try."

"I knew you would!" Casey said, patting his back as he turned toward the stage. "Oh, and Chip?"

"What?" he said.

"You can take the sock out of your pants," Casey whispered.

14

"EVERYBODY FINISH?" SAID MR. MICHAELS, bounding down the aisle after the end of rehearsal. "Everybody like?"

"Loved it!" Brianna replied, sealing the plastic cover on the one platter of leftover food. There wasn't a whole lot there. People had been picking at the food right up to the end of the rehearsal. Unfortunately everyone had made a mess, spilled food and drink all over the place. The DC members had to stay late to help Mr. Levin, Ms. Gunderson, and Mr. Ippolito clean up.

"Brianna, you come to Kostas Korner for dessert!" said Mr. Michaels. "Where is Harrison?"

"In the bathroom, I think." Brianna checked the clock: 6:32. Things had gone way late. She checked her schedule on her BlackBerry: *Home at 6:27, dinner until 6:45, calculus HW done by 7:05 . . .* —she was already off. She would have to redo the whole timetable. "I can't go tonight, Mr. Michaels, but thanks!"

As Mr. Michaels hustled off, Brianna dropped to her knees to help Dashiell clean a huge stain on the carpet. "I think Harrison is having a talk with Charles," Dashiell said. "He seemed embarrassed about what happened in the Green Room. I guess Charles found him with Reese in flagrante delicto."

Brianna dropped her cloth. "Um, Dashiell, you can't mean . . . you know . . . ?"

"Hooking up?" Dashiell replied. "Yes. Not that we should be surprised. Reese has been after him for a long time."

She couldn't believe this. This had to be a rumor. She picked up the cloth and began rubbing the stain. "You . . . got . . . *that* . . . right . . . "

"Of course, maybe it was a misunderstanding."

"Right . . . could be . . ."

"Charles has a vivid imagination."

"Yup . . . he does . . . "

"Although the way Reese is around Harrison, you never know."

"One . . . never knows . . . do one?"

"Um, I believe we have conquered the stain," Dashiell said. "You can probably stop."

Brianna lifted the cloth. She had nearly cleaned the color out of the carpet.

"Thanks for staying late, guys!" Mr. Levin called out.

"If you need to go, you've got my blessing."

6:41.

"Later, Dash," Brianna said, feeling numb. "Nice job tonight."

"Thank you for calling me Dash. You are one of the few."

She grabbed her coat and jogged out to the lobby. *Harrison and Reese . . . in the school?*

What if it wasn't a rumor? It shouldn't matter. It was Harrison's business and Reese's.

But it wasn't. It involved Brianna.

He had called her a *mistake*. Was he using her that night—as *practice* for Reese? Was that the mistake—he went too far? *Oops, sorry to totally turn your life upside down. Just needed to kick the tires on my babe skills before going after the real target.*

Through the glass front door, she could see Mr. Michaels pacing back and forth, talking on a cell phone. She didn't exactly want to face him in the mood she was in. Especially when his son was the cause. She could take the side entrance, off to the right.

She hurried in that direction, just beyond the men's room. The bathroom door had been propped open. As she walked by, she heard a scream from inside.

"Oh! OH! That is *so* Sal Mineo!"

It was Charles. He was standing behind Harrison, who leaned over a sink, looking into a mirror. Charles's hands were full of gel, and he was carefully examining Harrison's hairstyle.

The hair was like a sculpture, greased straight back at

the sides as if made of wax and piled high toward the front of his head, where it swooped upward like an ocean wave. You half expected a surfer to peek through. A perfect, picturesque curl hung down from the edge of the wave.

Brianna had the sudden, irrational urge to pull it all out with her bare hands.

"La Glaser!" Charles called.

Crap. Brianna scurried away, but it was too late.

"Where you going, girl?" said Charles, poking his head out of the door. "Welcome to Plaza Scopetta, your one-stop men's-room hair boutique. The decor lacks a certain flair, but please enter, we need your input!"

Brianna checked her watch. Harrison was looking decidedly unhappy to see her. "Looks great," she said.

"Curb your enthusiasm," Charles said. "*I* think it is to die for! The one thing he needs? Cheekbones. How about a little Johnny Depp uplift?"

He rubbed his fingers into a container of base. Standing behind Harrison, looking over his shoulder into the mirror, Charles applied the base to Harrison's cheek. He quickly rubbed it in, trying to create a shadow effect beneath his cheekbone.

"I like it," Harrison exclaimed, leaning close to the mirror.

"Don't touch or you'll get it all schmutzy!" Charles reached around to adjust the dark swoops of hair, singing to the tune of a song from the *Wizard of Oz* movie, "Touch-touch here, touch-touch there, and a bottle of la-di-da . . . wheeeee!"

"HARALAMBOS?"

The voice made Brianna jump.

She hadn't noticed Mr. Michaels walk up behind her. His face had an expression she had never seen before, to match the tone of voice she had never heard.

Harrison turned. His makeup suddenly looked garish, his hair too fussed over. "Hi, Dad," he said nonchalantly.

Charles darted over to the next sink and began washing his hands. "Hello, Mr. Michaels, we were just—"

"Haralambos, I see you outside, *now!*" Mr. Michaels said. As he headed for the door, he gave Charles a look that could peel paint. *"Vre maláka . . ."*

15

"THAT WAS *SO* WRONG, WHAT YOU JUST SAID, DAD," Harrison shouted as they got into the van, the cold air almost instantly freezing his moussed hair. "You have no idea."

"Pah. Tsarles no understand Greek, Haralambos." Mr. Michaels shifted uncomfortably in the driver's seat.

"He didn't have to! You were obvious, Dad. You hurt his feelings."

"Tsarles is good boy," Mr. Michaels said. "Clean. Respect the grown-ups. If I make him feel bad, I sorry."

"Okay, thanks," Harrison said. "I'll tell him."

"But he is not good friend for you. What *you* did? This bad thing. Look at you. A boy—with makeup!"

"Dad, it's a play. Theater. You wear makeup and do

your hair in the theater. The Greeks invented theater."

"The Greeks don't do like this, the boys with the boys!" Mr. Michaels said, pounding the steering wheel.

"Depends which history you read," Harrison replied.

"Haralambos!"

This conversation was veering into a place Harrison hated to go. A place he had always avoided. His dad's comments—the sexist and homophobic remarks, the winks and nudges, the snarky comments in Greek—it was like something from a parallel reality. Something you always explained away. Dad was Dad, he didn't mean it, it was cultural, it was just joking, blah blah blah.

Except when it wasn't.

"What Brianna thinking?" Mr. Michaels said, turning left onto the highway. "She nice girl. Beautiful. She looking at you and maybe she think you are . . . different."

"Different?"

"You know. Like Tsarles."

"You mean, funny, talented, smart, and loyal?" Harrison asked. "You mean, like a really good friend?"

"The girls, Haralambos, they like the real man. Not like the boys in the *musiki*. Talking about the makeup and the yeetee yeetee yeetee," Mr. Michaels said, raising his voice to a comical high pitch.

Harrison groaned. "Oh God, Dad. I don't know where to begin . . ."

"You, me—we Greeks. We like a little ooh-la-la! So many beautiful girls in you high school. They growing up. They ladies."

"With nice legs."

"Ooh-la-la."

"And the two big round *bezia*."

"Ho! *Etsi bravo!*"

Mr. Michaels laughed. He pulled into the Kostas Korner lot and parked near the kitchen entrance. Looking greatly relieved, he turned and gave Harrison a friendly punch in the arm. "Atta boy."

Harrison sighed and sat back deeply. His father hadn't caught the sarcasm at all.

Tuesday, January 22, 19:27:09

armchair_holiness: he didn't mean it, charles, he really likes you

SCOPASCETIC: *malaka is not a nice word, harrison. i looked it up on google*

armchair_holiness: he calls EVERYONE malaka

armchair_holiness: including guillermo . . .

armchair_holiness: the guy who supplies fish . . .

armchair_holiness: his own bro, my uncle elias (stavros's dad) . . .

SCOPASCETIC: *he calls his brother a faggot? it means faggot.*

armchair_holiness: it's just a word. he's old school. they're all into politics and sports. everything else is name-calling.

armchair_holiness: hair and makeup are not on the radar screen. kinda freaks him out.

armchair_holiness: he always puts his foot in his mouth, he feels bad about it

SCOPASCETIC: *sure was pleasant for me too*

SCOPASCETIC: *gtg, Harrison. one question—* *"armchair holiness"? what the? i never asked.*

armchair_holiness: anagram for harrison michaels.

SCOPASCETIC: *ah. well, thank you for the lesson in greek etiquette, now i gotta get my 8 hours*

SCOPASCETIC: *so I can sack troy*

armchair_holiness: kill a running boar with your bare hands like a real man heh heh

SCOPASCETIC: *:: spits, adjusts his jockstrap ::*

SCOPASCETIC: *toodles*

SCOPASCETIC: *i mean, later dude.*

SCOPASCETIC has signed off.

16

BRIANNA UNDID HER SCARF, WHICH WAS TOO loose against the bitter wind, then wrapped it around twice for extra warmth. She was a walking collection of Christmas gifts collected from her mom's business trips — pashmina scarf from India, handmade cable-knit wool sweater from Ireland, fur hat from China, thick down coat from Paramus, New Jersey, and a pair of insulated gloves that her dad liked to say came from the famous Spanish designer El L. Bean.

The walk felt good. The cold air was clearing her thoughts.

She would just drop by the diner for a short breakfast. It would be close to the end of Harrison's Saturday shift. They would take a walk afterward. Talk things out.

Brianna was mad, and he knew it. She hadn't been able to talk to him — really talk to him — all week. Since she found out about Reese. The rumor. Whatever it was. For days Harrison had been giving her looks — curious, frustrated looks. She owed him an explanation. And he *really* owed her one.

And maybe they would even talk abut the strange incident with his dad and Charles. Everything would have an explanation. Everything would be all right again. Somehow.

She needed everything to be all right.

Last night she had decided to go to sleep early. It hadn't worked. Her whole body had been too zingy to sleep, too used to being awake. Too much guilt over not doing work. She'd had to borrow a trazodone from her mom's medicine cabinet.

Note to self: Tell mom about the borrowed traz.

Shouldn't be a big deal. Mom had offered her the trazzies before on sleepless nights. Mom swore by them.

Brianna yawned.

As she walked past the school, she spotted a group of guys on the football field, by the grassy out-of-bounds area near the running track.

"Eleven-point-nine — you can do better than that, Newman!" The voice of Mr. Emmons, the track coach, rang out from the school football field.

Kyle was there. And Pete Newman and all the others, in shorts and T-shirts. *Laughing*, looking comfy and toasty warm, and in the company of a supposedly sane and trustworthy adult.

Guys were disturbing. Period. They disproved evolution (which was supposed to move toward *higher* beings, not lower) *and* intelligent design (because who with any intelligence would design them?).

As she descended a hill to the track, Kyle waved.

He was beautiful. He really was. And uncomplicated in his own way. Kyle was all about action, doing. Throw the javelin? Star in a show? Swim in the cold? Break a heart? He just *did*. With a smile and a shrug. No fuzziness. All instinct.

He was the anti-Harrison.

As she walked toward him, she wondered if she had made a colossal mistake not really *trying* with him. She'd had the chance. She could have made something of the night at the beach. Forced him a little. To stay connected. To make him be in the show, at gunpoint if necessary.

"It's like thirty degrees below zero," she said. "Aren't you cold?"

"Freezing," Kyle said. "But if I dressed right, I wouldn't look butch in front of Pete."

"Bite me, Taggart," said Pete Newman, bounding away toward a set of low hurdles.

"How's the show?" Kyle asked.

"Why?" Brianna said. "Have you changed your mind, say-yes say-yes say-yes?"

Kyle laughed. "Is that why you came here?"

"No, I'm on my way to see Harrison."

"Lucky Harrison." Kyle picked up a sleek, wooden javelin that was resting beside a long and narrow pathway made of sand. "Watch this."

Balancing the pole carefully in his hand, he stood at the edge of the sand path. The team immediately gathered around to watch.

"Start slow, Taggart, and keep it steady . . . " Coach Emmons said. "Eyes front. No bouncing . . . "

Kyle began jogging, his body slanted to the right, the javelin pulled back. With each step he picked up speed, until he was running fast. Then, just before the pathway ended, he heaved the javelin skyward.

"HEEEEYAHHH!"

It went unbelievably far. It seemed to go the whole length of the football field. When it finally landed, it broke the surface of the hard-packed dirt, where it stuck out at an angle.

"Measure that!" Coach Emmons commanded.

"Pull my finger," Pete said to Kyle, handing him one end of a tape-measure spool. As Kyle held tight to the tape, Pete jogged down the field toward the javelin. "One hundred ninety-four feet," he called out.

"Eight inches from the school record," Coach Emmons said.

"Yyyes!" Kyle exclaimed.

"It'll be fun to see what you can do with a totally good ankle," Coach Emmons replied. He glanced at his watch. "Okay, guys, let's do four laps and then a team meeting. We gotta get out of here."

Kyle was grinning. "See you later."

"Right," Brianna said.

The guys were shuffling out to the track. One by one they began to run. They were fast. All of them.

She watched Kyle. He wasn't the fastest, but she could tell he *would* be, if his ankle were 100 percent. As he rounded the turn, he gave her a little wave.

She waved back.

She hated this feeling. Like her life was one big centrifuge spinning out of control. And in the center, watching it all pass by with a carefree smile, was Kyle.

17

"IT'S CALLED SKORDALIA," DASHIELL SAID, PASSING
a plate with a whitish-gray lump across the table. "It is,
in my opinion, the peak of Greek cuisine. And on the
Saturday morning after the first week of rehearsals, it's
important to celebrate with the best!"

Shara Simmons gave it a dubious look. "How do you
eat it?"

"Like this." Dashiell grabbed a triangle of warm pita
bread out of a basket, dipped it in, and shoved it in his
mouth. "Mmm. Unique."

Shara followed his example tentatively, with a much
smaller portion. Her eyes bulged. "Gurp . . . "

"Tasty, huh?" Dashiell said.

"What's *in* this?" she asked.

"Potatoes," he said, scooping up another helping. "Raw garlic."

"Mostly garlic!" Shara reached for her glass of water.

"You quickly become accustomed to it," Dashiell assured her. "It's a specialty of the house. The food we had at rehearsal was the tip of the culinary iceberg. If you're going to live in Ridgeport, you must sample Kostas's finest."

A beefy hand clapped Dashiell on the shoulder. "You girlfriend like the skordalia?" Mr. Michaels said, beaming at them both.

"My g-girl — ?" Dashiell stammered. "Um, yes. Indeed, Mr. Michaels. She thoroughly enjoys it."

"Mmggll," said Shara, nodding, as she drank ice water.

"You ready for breakfast?" Mr. Michaels said. "You like scrambled eggs, waffles, pencakes, a Greek salad, maybe an omelet —"

"We will split a moussaka and a spanakopita," Dashiell said, "with a tzatziki on the side."

"We will?" Shara said.

Dashiell grinned. "Trust me."

"Bravo," Mr. Michaels said, scribbling the order on a slip of paper and heading for the kitchen. "I tell Harrison that you are here."

"Excellent," Dashiell said. "Please do."

Dashiell looked around for Harrison. By the kitchen, Mr. Michaels was handing his order slip to Niko the waiter. The two men exchanged some words loudly in Greek, gesturing toward their table.

"Don't you wish you knew what they were saying?" Shara asked.

"Probably, 'Give an extra big portion to that astonishingly beautiful girl,'" Dashiell said.

Shara smiled. And Dashiell had to fight from floating away from the table.

Brianna slipped in through the diner's side door. She slid into a booth just to Harrison's left and picked up a menu. His back was to her while he cleared a table. She could hear him muttering while he wiped up a big chocolate-shake spill.

When he finally turned, she peered over the top of the menu. "Boo."

"Oh. Hey, Bri," he said, looking startled. "What are you doing up this early?"

"We need to talk, Harrison," Brianna replied. "Plus, I'm hungry for a Spanish omelet and an orange juice. Then we can walk home after your shift."

"I thought we talked," Harrison said.

"Not about what happened in the Green Room."

"What happened in the Green Room?"

Brianna took a deep breath. "Don't play games with me. Charles saw you and Reese—"

"Warming up."

"According to Charles, it was *really* warm in there."

"He's joking, right? I *fell* into Reese. During a plié. I may be a good actor, but you know I'm a lousy dancer, okay? *That's* what Charles saw. Is that what you came here to do—accuse me?"

"*Fell* into Reese? Harrison, don't try to game me."

"Believe whatever you want, Brianna. I don't have time to argue."

She took a deep breath. It was almost too stupid an excuse *not* to be true. "Sorry, Harrison. I—I didn't mean to stress you out."

"Yeah . . . I didn't mean to snap." Harrison quietly sat in the seat opposite her. "It's not you, it's Dad. Do you know what he just did? Look over by the window. You see Dashiell—with Shara? Okay, Dashiell's like the smartest guy on the planet, right? Well, my dad takes his order and gives it to Niko. Niko asks him who's it for, and Dad says, '*O mavros*.' Loud enough for Dashiell to hear. '*O mavros*'!"

Brianna craned her neck. At a table by the window she could see the back of Dashiell's head. "And that means . . . ?"

Harrison lowered his voice. "*Mavro* means 'black.' So he's saying 'the black.' Not Dashiell. *The black*."

"Ew," Brianna said. "But . . . why? I mean, your dad *likes* Dashiell. And Dashiell likes him. Is he a racist?"

"Racist, sexist, homophobic—it depends on his mood! He did the same kind of thing with Charles. Sometimes I just think it's his shtick, you know? The Kosta Michaels Show—'God bless America' and all. Make everybody laugh. They have this weird sense of humor—Dad and the waiters. They love to say bad things in Greek—sometimes right in people's faces. With a smile. Like he'll tell the fish supplier, 'You have a penis in your ear' in Greek, like he's giving him a compliment. It makes Niko and George crack up. The fish guy doesn't know. He smiles back and says thanks."

"That is so *My Big Fat Greek Wedding.*"

"Old school. Totally. It's like these guys have a shorthand. Anyone who's black—*mavro.* Anyone who's gay, or seems gay, or even just gets them mad for any reason—*maláka.* Do they hate people? Maybe. I didn't *used* to think so. But sometimes he seems to really mean it."

Suddenly the kitchen door swung open. Mr. Michaels barged out, wearing his long wool coat and talking on his cell.

His face was red. "HARRISON!" he called out, not breaking stride.

"What the—?" Harrison stood up from his seat and ran. By the door, they talked Greek, fast and furious.

As Mr. Michaels ran out to the parking lot, Harrison stood and watched. His shoulders were slumped.

Brianna cautiously walked up beside him. Dashiell and Shara, having seen the commotion, had walked up, too. "Harrison?" Brianna said.

Harrison sank down onto a stool by the cash register. "It's my uncle Taso," he said softly. "Dad's older brother. He just died of a heart attack."

"Oh, Harrison . . ." Brianna took his hand. "Your cousin Stavros's father?"

"No, thank God," Harrison said. "That's Elias, his younger brother. Taso was older."

"Were you close?" Shara asked.

"No," Harrison said. "He and Dad had a fight, years ago, and they stopped talking to each other."

"So maybe that eases things," Dashiell suggested.

Harrison shook his head. "It makes it worse." He sighed. "The guilt. He is going to be impossible to live with."

Saturday, January 26, 17:02:43

armchair_holiness: hey, stavros, u hear? about uncle taso?

stavinfexshun: yup. dad went 2 chicago.

armchair_holiness: i cant believe it.

stavinfexshun: hes been sick for ages.

armchair_holiness: i didn't know

stavinfexshun: guess yr dad didn't tell you. or maybe he didnt know either

stavinfexshun: those 2 dudes hated each other.

armchair_holiness: never understood why. did ur dad ever tell u?

stavinfexshun: money thing. uncle taso is rich. real estate.

stavinfexshun: the younger bros were jealous. my dad too.

stavinfexshun: i think taso lent yr dad $$ when KK wasnt doing so great.

armchair_holiness: did my dad pay him back?

stavinfexshun: i think so. i dont know. something happened.

stavinfexshun: my dad doesnt like to talk about it.

stavinfexshun: its a greek thing

18

"DEVON?"

"Huh?"

"It's Brianna. Hi, I know it's Sunday night. I'm sorry. It's just—I was at Kostas Korner yesterday and Kostas's brother in Chicago died and I got really upset but I couldn't even talk to Harrison after that because he was even more upset and then I went home and basically I haven't slept much this weekend because I've been working ever since and the time has just flown, so it still feels like Saturday afternoon—"

"Whoa, whoa. Easy. Slow down. 'Sup? Why are you calling me?"

"Were you sleeping?"

"It's like three in the morning, Brianna."

"Two forty-nine. I'm sorry, Devon. Like I said, I'm so out of it. Forget it. I'll see you tomorrow—"

"No, no, it's okay. Tell me. I'm awake now."

"I did two practice SATs? And they took me all night. I totally screwed the first one. But the second was better."

"On a *Sunday night?*"

"Exactly. But . . . it was like one-thirty and I was like *oh crap, I forgot to do my homework!*"

"Oh."

"I did the calc, that was easy, and I studied for the English quiz, but it's the history essay. It's huge. Like fifteen percent of the semester grade. So I'm tanked up with caffeine but I'm shaking. I can't think straight."

"You'll be okay, Brianna. You have the highest grade in the class. In the school. You have nothing to worry about."

"Thanks, Devon. That's really nice. I don't have the highest, though—I think Caleb does. I mean, I wasn't calling you for a pep talk, but it was nice."

"Well . . . my parents are asleep. So you could come over if you want, Brianna. If you need something to help out."

"That would be okay? I'll pay you back."

"I have some uppers. But you're already hyper. The other stuff just makes you groggy. I don't know . . . Ritalin?"

"Yeah? I never tried—"

"It works. Look, Brianna, you have to be really really quiet when you come over. My dad's not such a sound sleeper. The back door."

"Just this one time, Devon, okay?"

"Right."

"You're awesome. Thanks sooooo much."

"Whatever. Just get here fast."

"I'll be right over."

armchair_holiness: u there, bri?

armchair_holiness: i cant sleep

armchair_holiness: u2?

armchair_holiness: hello

armchair_holiness: brianna

armchair_holiness: ru in the bathroom?

armchair_holiness: im here.

armchair_holiness has signed off 3:07:34 A.M.

19

"WHUH—WHAT?" BRIANNA SAT UP STRAIGHT.
Someone was asking her a question. And expecting an
answer.

For a moment she didn't know where she was. Her chin
was propped up on the flats of her two hands, elbows on
the desk, her fingers shielding her eyes to make it look like
she wasn't asleep, just deep in thought.

The clock came into focus first, and then the face of
Mr. Brotman, her math teacher. "Problem 13a," he said.
"The differential equation."

Brianna sat up and opened her notebook. Her back
ached and her teeth hurt. The writing was blurred. She
blinked hard, squeezing the sleep from her eyes.

It was her English assignment. "Oh. Oops. Wait . . . "

Mr. Brotman nodded at the desk behind her. "Michael?"

"Forty-three a to the fourth plus six b to the third minus eighteen c squared plus seven d," said Michael Herrara.

"Perfect," said Mr. Brotman.

Brianna fumbled in her book bag. It was crammed. She yanked out her math notebook, releasing three pens, two Kit Kat wrappers, and a graphing calculator onto the floor.

Mr. Brotman knelt to help her pick up everything.

"Sorry! Sorry!" she said. "I'll do the next problem."

"Don't worry," Mr. Brotman said, handing her the calculator. "You just get yourself settled."

Brianna flipped open her notebook with a sinking feeling. Class participation was *huge* in Mr. Brotman's class. At least 15 percent of the grade. And if you were missing a homework assignment, you lost a point off your average.

She couldn't afford a point. Mainly because Caleb was a math genius. Perfect scores across the board.

The thing was, she had gotten the answer right. If she had only been awake . . .

"Mr. Brotman?" she said, waving her hand. "Mr. B?"

"God, will you chill?" said Michael.

"Would you shut up?" Brianna snapped.

RINNNNG!

The ending bell startled her. She stood and packed up. "Can I do two tomorrow—to compensate?" she asked.

"Sure, Brianna," Mr. Brotman replied. "You have nothing to worry about."

"If you can stay awake," Michael muttered.

"Your fly's open," Brianna replied, "but no one will notice."

She headed into the hallway. Next period was lunch.

She couldn't afford to doze again. She needed hydration. Carbs. Energy. She would need to eat fast, because lunch was the time she had scheduled for memorizing Rizzo's lines.

The role wasn't as bad as Brianna had thought it might be. In fact, given her state of mind, playing a tough, sarcastic, bitter, downtrodden, troublemaking underachiever suited her just fine.

"Yo, Brianna! Dude!" It was Devon, strolling toward her with a big grin. "You look like hell."

"I bet you say that to all the girls," Brianna replied.

"Get any sleep last night?" he said, falling into step with her.

"Didn't need to. I was able to make it all up in Brotman's class. Slept like a baby."

As they rounded the corner, he lowered his voice. "You don't have to be like this."

"I do not need criticism—"

"No, I mean it, Brianna. You don't need to feel so strung out. I can help you."

"Help?" Brianna stopped short. "You mean . . . *help*? Like the way you helped me last night?"

Devon smiled. "That's what friends are for."

The conversation didn't seem real. "So . . . you're saying, you have something that will keep me awake. Right now. I—I can't believe we're talking about this."

"No worries." Devon began backing away down the hallway. "You need me, you know where I am. Feel better, okay?"

Brianna turned. The girls' room was just down the hall. She went inside and caught a whiff of cigarette smoke. Across the room, three girls were puffing away in front of the window.

Holding back her gag reflex, she ducked into a stall. She bolted the door behind her and leaned up against it.

Outside the girls had burst into song. Some stupid Christina Aguilera tune. She hated it. She blocked it out until they were done, until they headed out into the hallway and the bell rang for next period.

She would stay there for a minute or two, and then go to lunch.

Standing up, propped against the metal door, she drifted off to sleep.

20

"LET'S GO, GUYS!" CASEY CALLED OUT FROM behind the curtain stage left. "Come on, we haven't even rerun the 'Beauty School Dropout' scene after that first time. Let's do it—now!"

She crossed her fingers. It was only Tuesday, first rehearsal of the week, but the number had been a disaster. Sammy Wilkens, playing Teen Angel, had come down with a sore throat the week before. Even though he'd had the weekend to rest, he wasn't any better.

As the cast gathered on the stage, she heard a sickening thump from backstage. "Is everything okay?" she asked.

Charles and the Charlettes were gathered around a replica of a fifties-style convertible hot rod. Painted a metallic red, with the words GREASED LIGHTNING along the side and long fins extending from the back, it was just big enough for two people to climb into.

"Everything is dandy," Charles said, "except that our motor fell out. See, someone had the bright idea that the car should move by remote control. Hence we have a motor."

Gabe Hirsch, one of the Charlettes, lifted a large mechanical contraption from inside the car's hood. "We just have to strengthen the support. The axles are holding steady and the driveshaft didn't get damaged. It's really easy to do, Charles."

Charles gave Casey a look. "Robotics Club," he said. "They think anything's easy."

"WHERE'S OUR SOLOIST?" cried Mr. Levin from the house.

Casey peeked out. The rear door of the auditorium opened and Sammy Wilkens rushed in. He ran to the stage and pointed to his neck, which was wrapped in a thick acrylic scarf. "It's still not better," he croaked.

"That's okay," Ms. Gunderson said. "Sing softly. Peter will use the damper pedal."

Sammy climbed the stage and started to sing.

Talk.

Whisper.

Peter was playing the piano so lightly his fingers were barely touching the keys.

Within a few bars Sammy had stopped singing entirely and was just going through the motions Reese had taught him. Casey felt for him. There wasn't much you could do about laryngitis.

WHACK! WHACK! WHACK! WHACK!

"Charlettes! Please! Hammers are for the hallway!" Charles shouted.

"Oy, the *nebbishes,* I tried to tell them," said Vijay, shoving Gabe.

"Does *anyone* have a suggestion for how to fit the car through the door?" Gabe asked.

"Gentlemen, ladies, and Charlettes," Dashiell said. "Please keep the noise level to a dull roar."

"Places for 'Beauty School'!" Casey called out.

As the actors took their marks Brianna paced. "Casey, I'm worried. We have to call a meeting and replace Sammy."

"It's just laryngitis," Casey said. "He'll get better."

"Have you heard him warming up?" Brianna replied. "It's not laryngitis. It's technique. He makes himself hoarse. He needs a voice teacher."

"He'll work with Ms. Gunderson and Peter," Casey said.

"You have to be tougher, Casey," Brianna insisted. "You won't hurt his feelings—look at him, he's *asking* to be let off the hook. And we don't have the time to waste. Better to replace him now than have to train somebody at the last minute. We can get Harrison to do the dirty work. He knows how to fire people without making them feel bad. Where is Harrison anyway?"

"He said he had to go shopping for a suit," Casey said. "But he should be here any minute."

"A *suit?*" Brianna said. "He didn't tell me that. Why can't he do that on the weekend, instead of Tuesday?"

"He has to go to Chicago on the weekend," Casey replied. "Maybe he needs to leave it for alterations."

WHACK! WHACK! WHACK!

Casey flinched.

"Charle-e-e-ettes! This is not wood shop!" Charles cried out.

"Will you guys knock it off!" Brianna screamed.

Vijay covered his ear. "Such a *tsurris*."

"Enough with the Yiddish! You are *not* Jewish, Vijay!" Brianna said, storming off the stage. "What is with you— *all* of you! This is a play. It's serious business!"

The wings fell silent. "What was that all about?" Vijay asked.

"Egos make the world go 'round, boys and girls," Charles said. "Work now. Discussion later."

As the Charlettes went back to the hot rod, Charles leaned closer to Casey. "Um, any ideas what turned on the diva switch?"

Casey shrugged. "She has a lot on her mind, Charles."

"So do we all, darling," Charles said, heading backstage. "Charlettes, hurry and fix that thing, will you, so you can drive me home?"

Casey looked out into the auditorium. Brianna was off to the side, scowling, her cell phone pressed to her ear.

She was worried about Brianna. Brianna hadn't looked well lately. Like she was fighting the flu, or mono. This morning at her locker she had barely said a word.

It was the pressure. From homework, from the college process, from her personal life. Too much pressure lowered your body's resistance. Casey knew the feeling.

"OOOOOHH . . . OOOHHHH . . . " came the sound of the chorus of "Beauty School Dropout." It was strange without the soloist singing.

Poor Sammy was sitting off to the side, watching. He did look miserable. Maybe Brianna was right. He might be happy to leave the show.

As the number ended, Casey checked her clipboard. "Summer Lovin'" was next on the schedule. "Okay, I need Sandy and Danny!" she called out.

Shara was already onstage in the "Beauty School" number. But Harrison was nowhere to be seen.

"DANNY ZUKO?" Casey repeated.

"He's probably in one of the practice rooms," said Jamil, one of the Burger Palace Boys. "I'll go look."

"Tell him to hurry," Casey said. She checked her watch. Everything was behind schedule. The karma of this whole rehearsal was off. Charles was arguing with the Charlettes, Brianna was arguing with Dashiell, Shara was defending Dashiell.

Her cell phone began to vibrate in her pocket. Probably Ripley in the projection booth.

As Casey reached into her pocket, a motor coughed to life backstage. Charles screamed.

The stage left curtain began to bulge. From under the curtain came *Greased Lightning*. It was moving slowly, but part of its chrome trim caught the edge of the fabric. With a loud rip, a chunk of curtain came loose, which draped over the top of the car as it emerged onto the stage, followed by five Charlettes.

"What the—?" said Mr. Levin, who had walked onstage to give notes.

The car rolled across the stage, picking up speed. It knocked aside Sammy's stool, swerving upstage and taking out a prop table and the wooden frame for the soda counter of the Burger Shop.

As Mr. Levin moved toward it, Gabe leaped into the car headfirst. It crashed through the canvas of a half-painted flat and plunged into a rack of costumes.

Buffered by the fabric, it hit the back wall of the stage and stopped, its engine whining as Gabe struggled to sit upright and flick the switch off.

"What the heck was that?" Mr. Levin said. "Are you okay?"

Gabe turned. He shook loose a fake mink fur that had landed on his head. He was beaming. "It works, Mr. Levin. *It works!*"

Casey plopped down into a seat. She buried her face in her hands. Her heart was pumping overtime.

They would need a new flat. A new curtain. Massive repairs on the costumes. Maybe a rebuilt car. *If* they were lucky and the school didn't close the show for liability issues. She knew of a school in Connecticut where that had happened.

This is it. This has got to be the worst that can happen.

"Casey?" said Jamil, kneeling beside her. "Are you okay?"

"Fine," she replied, forcing a smile. "Did you get Harrison from the practice room?"

"We can't find him."

"Really? But he was just here—"

She thought back. No. He wasn't just here. She realized she hadn't seen him at all during this rehearsal.

Reaching into her pocket, she pulled out her cell phone: 1 MISSED CALL showed on the screen.

She hit the display button and read the result:

MICHAELS, HARRISON.

21

"DAMN," HARRISON MURMURED, LOOKING AT his cellphone screen: 3 MISSED CALLS. All from Brianna.

He had tried to contact Casey to tell her he would be late, but she hadn't picked up. How had he missed the calls from Brianna?

He had been too busy arguing with his dad at Syms, that's how. Shopping for a funeral suit with his dad had to go down on the list of Top Ten Dreary Experiences of All Time. Right up there with walking on ground glass and drinking prune juice.

No use calling the DC now. Harrison pocketed the phone, hung his new clothes in his bedroom closet, and headed downstairs. "Later!" he called out.

His dad appeared at the bottom of the stairs, stepping out of the kitchen. "Where you going?" he demanded.

"To what's left of rehearsal," Harrison replied, stepping around him.

"Rehearsal? What you mean rehearsal?"

Harrison rubbed his forehead. "Um, the play?"

"Harrison, your uncle died."

"Right. I know that. That's why we went shopping."

His dad gave him a wounded look. "Your uncle die and you no care?"

"I do care. But what am I supposed to do, Dad? There's nothing I can do here."

"He is family! No *musiki* when family die. No dancing. Is very bad. You have to be quiet. You have to respect. Is Greek tradition."

"You never told me that. Is this like sitting *shivah?* Like the Jewish tradition? You sit at home for a week and have visitors?"

"Is *mnimosino*. You respect for forty days!"

"*Forty?*"

Mr. Michaels nodded. "You respect, every day. And then we have big service in church—"

"Wait. You're saying I can't go to rehearsal for *forty days?*"

"He die Saturday, so forty, thirty-nine, thirty-eight—"

Harrison shook his head. "But—but I can't do that—"

"Thirty-seven days, Haralambos."

"I—I don't believe this. Dad, I don't even *know* Uncle Taso. I haven't seen him in years! I don't remember what he looks like."

"He's my brother. I have picture."

"But the funeral is this weekend. We're flying to

Chicago for one day and then it'll be over. What's with *forty days*? The show will be *over* in forty days."

"The funeral, it happens right away. The *mnimosino*, in forty days. Two services. Both very important." His dad took a big tub of hummus from the fridge. "You hungry? Sit."

"But, Dad, I can't just quit! I'm playing the lead. I'm the club president! Am I supposed to stay home from school, too? Sit in my room for six weeks?"

"Haralambos," Mr. Michaels said, taking Harrison by the wrist. "The show is good. You very good singer. Actor, too. Is fun. But is no arithmetic. Is no *historia*, physics. If show still going in thirty-seven days, you be in it. If not, you do next one. You tell them, 'My uncle die and I have to do *mnimosino* with my family.' They will understand."

Harrison pulled his arm loose. He had heard his dad say odd things before, but this was insane. "Mom!" he called back upstairs. *"Mom!"*

Mrs. Michaels came to the top of the stairs. She looked tired, her salt-and-pepper hair pulled back into a bun. She had just changed out of her silk blouse and skirt into an RHS sweatshirt and jeans. She had been born in New York City and spoke perfect, educated, uninflected English — unless she was upset, when a slightly honking New York accent flavored her speech. At this moment, after a long day working behind the cash register at Kostas Korner, followed by shopping for black clothing, she was halfway to Brooklyn. "What are you two fighting about now?"

Harrison raced up the stairs. She would put some sense into this discussion. She would set his dad straight. She did not have one foot in the old world. She did not grow up riding donkeys and milking goats and passing down traditions. "Talk to Dad, please. He's telling me I can't be in the play until the forty-day memorial service!"

She cocked her head. "Oh?"

"That is not true! I no say, *can't be in play!*" Mr. Michaels protested. "I say, forty days! *Thirty-seven!*"

His wife gave him a dubious look. "That doesn't make sense. I've never heard of this tradition."

"This is what we do all the time, when I growing up in Tsitsifies!" Mr. Michaels said. "When my grandfather die, we do not listen to the *musiki*. We stop the dancing."

"*Vre* Kosta, be reasonable . . . " said Mrs. Michaels.

"It's not the same, Dad!" Harrison said. "It's a totally different thing. Look, call the church. Ask Father Vasili. I bet he'll tell you—"

His dad's face turned red. "I no have to call Father Vasili! In Greece the children listen! If my father saw me dancing and singing like *koritsi*—"

"Like a *koritsi*? Did you say that? Did you say *like a girl*?" Harrison laughed out loud. Suddenly this was all making sense. It wasn't about Uncle Taso at all. "I see what you're doing. You're making this up. To keep me out of the Drama Club."

"Making up *mnimosino*?" Mr. Michaels thundered.

"Your father caters all your opening rehearsals, Harrison," his mom reminded him. "He lets your friends eat even if they don't have money—"

"He never comes to the shows!" Harrison said.

"That's because he's *working*," his mom replied.

"That's because he hates the idea of me being an actor!"

"Harrison!" his mom said scoldingly.

His father stood from the table. His eyes were red. "We raise you to think of *family*! Not like the *Amerikaniki*!" He made a fist, thumping his chest as he said, "Me! Me! Me! All the same. Me! Selfish. Now you, too! Everything is about what Harrison want!"

"What *I* want?" Harrison looked him straight in the eye. "This is not about me. This is about *you*. You never liked me doing theater. You thought I would just grow out of it. But you freaked the other night. You saw Charles helping me with hair gel and makeup! We were having fun. But it scared you. My son, the *maláka*! All of a sudden I was hanging out with the wrong people. So when Uncle Taso died—sweet! A perfect excuse."

"*You talk to me like that!*" Mr. Michaels's fists were balled up. "You say I make up tradition. You think I am so stupid. That I worry you are going to turn into *maláka*. You are no Michalakis!"

"Please, Kosta," Harrison's mom said, gently touching her husband's arm.

"Right. I am no Michalakis. I'm Michaels!" Harrison replied. "It's on my birth certificate. And who changed the name? Who made it American? *You* did! You can't have it both ways, Dad. Even if people in Tsitsifies weep and cry and burn their iPods when someone dies. Even if they roll up the goddamn sidewalks, *you're not there anymore*."

Harrison barged across the kitchen and grabbed the car keys off the table.

"HARALAMBOS!" Mr. Michaels's voice boomed so loud Harrison could feel it through the floor. "You go to rehearsal, you no come back!"

"Fine!"

"You live in street. I have no son!"

"I have no father!"

"*Will you two fools stop it!*" Mrs. Michaels screamed. She placed herself between them, her face strained and angry. "You are exactly the same, both of you!"

"I can't live in the same house with him," Harrison said.

"You have exactly one and a half more years, Harrison," his mom said. "And then you're on your own. This isn't that big a deal, Harrison. It would obviously mean a lot to your father, and that counts for something, doesn't it?"

"Mom? Are you joking?"

"You have brains and achievement. Ambition. You yourself said you didn't like *Grease* anyway. Use the time to get your grades up. Do you really want to run away and give up your education—over something like this? So *trivial*? We trust you and believe in you. We want you to do the things that give you fulfillment, whatever they are. But you live in this house. And it's not a democracy. We can discuss rules, but in the end, your father and I set them. And sometimes we don't agree, sometimes they're not fair or fun. Rules are like that."

"You're backing him?" Harrison said.

"We were married in the Greek church," his mom

replied, "and you were baptized there. If you refrain from being in a show for forty days of your life because that's the proper way to respect your dad's brother, then so be it."

"Thirty-seven," Mr. Michaels muttered.

Harrison stared at her in disbelief. He thought she would take his side. But she was totally under his dad's thumb. Like everybody else.

He wanted to bolt. He wanted to make them cry. To make them eat their words. But Mom was right. Running was worse than staying. He could go to Stavros's, but they would make him go home eventually. He could hitch across the country, but if he was lucky, he would get as far as Pittsburgh before the money ran out. He could try to work, but without a diploma, he would be looking at a Fryolator all his life.

They had him.

Harrison looked at his father. Into those close-set, stubborn, triumphant eyes. He knew it. Kostas Michaels knew he had won.

But he hadn't.

"Okay, then," Harrison said, slapping the keys down on the table. "I will mourn Uncle Taso and go to the services. I will not be in the show. I will go to school. I will work at the diner. No play. No rehearsing. No after-school activity at all for forty days."

"Bravo," Mr. Michaels grumbled.

"But," Harrison said, heading up the stairs, "I will not be living here."

"Oh, Harrison, what are you talking about?" his mom said wearily.

Without another word, Harrison marched upstairs to his room. He emptied his backpack on the floor. He opened his dresser and grabbed some twenties he had stashed from tips. Then he stuffed into his pack some underwear and socks, a few T-shirts, a pair of jeans, and his cell-phone charger. He was wearing everything else he needed. He slung the pack over one shoulder, quickly zipped his laptop into its case and slung that, too, then walked downstairs.

"See you," he said, walking toward the front door.

"HARALAMBOS, YOU STAY RIGHT HERE!" shouted his father.

Harrison whirled around. "You got what you wanted, Dad. Forty days of respect. Quiet. No music. And now you'll have no arguing either. Because I won't be here. That's my end of the bargain."

"YOU DO THIS AND YOU NEVER COME BACK!" Mr. Michaels said.

"Kosta, don't be ridiculous!" Harrison's mom said. "You created this. Where will you be, Harrison?"

Harrison shrugged. "Haven't figured that out yet. I'll let you know."

He turned, walked quickly through the living room, and left through the front door.

22

Tuesday, January 29, 5:49 P.M.
From: <scopascetic@rport.li.com>
To: <CHARLETTES_AND_FRIENDS>
Subject: PARTY! FUN! ETC
Hi kidzzzzzz,
   a reminder! pls send right away to EVERYONE you know!!!!!

COME TO A BACKSTAGE PARTY THIS SATURDAY, FEB 2!!
JOIN THE CHARLETTES FOR REFRESHMENTS AND MUSIC WHILE WE REPAIR COSTUMES & FLATS & MAKE A MOVING PLATFORM TO BE USED IN THE GREASED LIGHTNING NUMBER!

it's really about work, but don't make it sound like that!! we REEEEALLY need a lot of people if we want this show to work!

XOXOXO,
CS
ps. btw i am sending this from backstage during tues rehearsal and the show already looks FAB!

"He quit!" Brianna said, rushing out of the auditorium door and through the front lobby.

Sitting on the lobby floor, Casey looked up from her script. She was running lines with Barry "Kenickie" Squires on a bench. "Who quit?" she called out.

Brianna barged out through the front door without answering, coatless and holding a cell phone to her ear. "Harrison."

Casey handed the script to Barry. It was time to go home anyway. "Work on it tonight. I can help you again tomorrow."

She ran into the auditorium, grabbed her coat and Brianna's, and raced outside.

Brianna was halfway up the block on Porterfield Street. "What happened?" Casey said, handing Brianna her coat.

"I'm going to kill him," Brianna said, putting on her coat as she walked. "He left a message. His dad said he can't do the show. Some Greek tradition. Something to do with his uncle's death. So Harrison's going to live with someone else for forty days, just to get back at him. *Can you believe this crap?*"

"Wait—he's running away from home?" Casey said.

"No. He says he'll move in with someone. But he can't be in the show. He can't rehearse. He can't stay after school."

"That's some tradition," Casey said.

"It's bull," Brianna replied. "It's Harrison's dad being . . . being old school and stubborn. And the rest of the world can just go suck a doughnut."

"Maybe it's a misunderstanding. It will all blow over."

"Ohhhhh, no. No way. Not with those two. I just know Harrison put up a fight. And that would make Mr. Michaels dig in more."

"But he's such a sweet guy—"

"You don't know him, Casey. He and Harrison—they're exactly alike, stubborn and thick. They always have fights like this. Even when Harrison was three. He came to my house, all angry. He was going to be my twin brother and call himself Harrison Glaser. That's the thing. Harrison just makes it worse. Even if his dad *could* be persuaded, Harrison just gets sucked in. It's like a power play. Now what? What are we going to do without a Danny?"

"Maybe we should just wait until they work it out."

"This is the *Spring Musical*, Casey!" Brianna shouted. "It's not some game. We can't wait for those two to grow up. What if it doesn't happen? Harrison says he's not coming back, fine. Replace him. Keep the show moving. The world does not revolve around Harrison Michaels!"

Casey took a deep breath. Already her stage manager's mind was working. "This means scheduling new auditions."

"Other people were good," Brianna said. "Devon was good."

"Yeah, but come on, Brianna, Devon is . . . "

Brianna stopped. "What?"

"Well, he wouldn't be a good fit."

"What is he, Casey? A skank? A druggie? Tell me."

"We have to think about group chemistry, Brianna."

Brianna's face broke into a smile. "Chemistry . . . ?" she said brightly.

Casey recognized a musical-trivia-challenge moment when she saw one. With Brianna you had to be prepared at any time. "Yeah, *chemistry*," she shot back.

"Very good," Brianna said. "And it's from . . . ?"

"*Guys and Dolls*," Casey said.

"During?"

"Dialogue in the middle of 'I'll Know When My Love Comes Along.'"

"You're good, Case." They fell in step, turning right at the next corner, toward Brianna's house.

"Let's sleep on it, Brianna, okay?" Casey said. "Give him a few days. I know you're mad, but—"

"No, Casey," Brianna said. "Look, I know Harrison. If anyone understands him, it's me. But we have a show to run. We have to take him at his word. I can't be worrying about this. I am behind in my homework, about to flunk every subject, taking the SAT and doing the prep course, and writing my college essay. This can't be all about Harrison."

Casey groaned. "Oh God, the college essay. Don't we, like, have another year for that?"

"It's early. My mom hired a coach for me, someone she knows from Harvard. He has a schedule. First draft in February, then we keep adding and shaping throughout the year. Building on experiences. Shaping a narrative. Finding my story. Building the brand and selling it to the market, because that's what it is. The brand of Brianna. This is how you have to think. Junior year, Case. Comes around once. You either hit the big time, grab one of the slots, or you're writing rain checks at Rite Aid. Which is why we have to find a new Danny Zuko."

"Uh, right," Casey said with a confused smile. "I think I get the connection."

"And that doesn't even take into consideration the schoolwork. I can't be thinking of all of this—and Harrison's ego—when I have twelve footnoted pages on Bren Fanklin due next week. Ben Franklin. Oh God, I need a nap." Brianna sighed. "Maybe fifteen minutes, and then I have to get to work."

"Hot chocolate would be good. It has endorphins."

"I prefer mine with marshmallows. Come over. We'll make some."

Brianna's house was a long walk, but Casey stayed with her. It was an instinct. Brianna needed company. The news about Harrison scared her, but she wasn't admitting it.

It scared Casey, too.

The town of Ridgeport changed totally in the Heights section. A century ago it was the grounds of a famous shipping magnate's estate, hundreds of acres stretching to the sea. Now it was rolling lawns and mansions, nestled in wooded areas of pine and maple. Casey loved to visit the Glasers. Living on Yale Drive with her mom in a snug little aluminum-sided cottage was cozy, but she envied the fact that Brianna could look out her window into misty fields, instead of peering into the bedroom of ten-year-old twins who liked to whack each other with SpongeBob toys and make pig faces out the window.

Brianna let them both in the house and called out, "I'm home! Celebrate! Let out the prisoners!"

As she dropped her pack on the living room sofa, a high-pitched voice cried out, "Brianna! Watch!"

Colter, her five-year-old brother, appeared at the top of the staircase and lay down on the curved mahogany banister. He looked a little like a small beached walrus, Casey thought as he began to slide down.

"Colter, you're not supposed to—" Brianna cried out.

"Ahh . . . ahhhhhh . . ." Colter tilted to the outside of the banister and began to fall. "AAAGGHHHHH!"

Running forward, Brianna reached out and caught him. The two landed in a heap on the new Turkish rug.

"Colter Glaser, how many times have I told you—" shouted his nanny, Siobhan, from upstairs.

"Colter, that hurt!" Brianna yelled.

"Waaaaaghhh!" screamed Colter.

Racing downstairs, Siobhan whisked the wailing boy away. Brianna stood, holding her forehead. "Shoot me, okay, Casey?" she said. "Relieve me from this sucky life."

As Brianna staggered up the stairs, Casey could see how tired she really was. Her knees looked as if they were held in place by rubber bands.

Brianna's room was huge, looking out over an expanse of back lawn that ended in a forested glade. Everything was neat and organized except the top of Brianna's desk. It was a disaster. Obviously the housekeeper was not allowed to touch that.

Brianna plopped herself on the bed and shut her eyes.

"Maybe I should go," Casey said, "and let you sleep."

"Yeah, maybe . . . " Brianna replied. She sat up and gave Casey a wry smile. "Siobhan can drive you back."

"I'll walk. It's not that far."

"We'll do the hot chocolate tomorrow, okay? When I'm caught up? Sorry I made you come all this way . . . "

"No problem," Casey replied. "I wanted to."

Brianna reached for the alarm and began pushing buttons. "IM me as soon as you get home. You'll see. I'll be perfect again."

Her head sank back onto the pillows, her voice drifted off, and a moment later so did she, her forehead creased with worry, her eyes pinched shut against the light of the setting sun.

Casey pulled down the blinds. An eye mask lay crumpled on Brianna's desk against the wall, on top of a pile of junk. Casey picked it up, untangling the fabric-covered elastic bands from a tangle of rubber bands.

As she lifted the mask, an envelope flipped over and its contents spilled out.

In the upper left, the return address, *Ridgeport Attendance Office*, was crossed out. Brianna's name had been scribbled on the center.

Four large round white pills lay on the table, along

with a handwritten message on a Post-it note, its adhesive strip folded on itself.

Don't say I never gave you nothing.
You will be glad you have these.
They're on the house.
A secret admirer.

23

Wednesday, January 30, 5:49 P.M.
armchair_holiness: *kc? u there?*
changchangchang: harrison????????????? where ru?
armchair_holiness: *you know craig weigel? he lives on walker street.*
changchangchang: ru ok? brianna told me what happened. i didn't see u in school today.
armchair_holiness: *i wasn't there. but I will be tmw. i'm fine. the weigels are cool. craig is my oldest non-DC friend. he saw me after i left my house yesterday. he was driving around & asked what was up*
armchair_holiness: *next thing i know his parents*

are inviting me to stay. i can use the top bunk.
craig's brother is at kenyon
changchangchang: nice. b says you cant be in the
show
armchair_holiness: *no. she wants to kill me, i*
know. but i cant do anything about it.
changchangchang: she is very stressed.
armchair_holiness: *what else is new. look. i tried*
to im her but she must have blocked me. tell her i'll
be in school tmw. pls tell her i want to talk to her
changchangchang: ok
armchair_holiness: *i started this long email to*
everybody. im going to send it tonight, so everybody
hears my end of the story b4 i see them tmw.
changchangchang: um . . . y dont u sleep on it?
armchair_holiness: *why? tmw will b too late*
changchangchang: i mean u might change ur
mind
armchair_holiness: *sorry, kc. It's beyond my*
control.

"You're *here*, Harrison," Brianna said. "It's Thursday, and you've only missed one rehearsal. You are standing one floor up and a mere two hundred or so yards from the auditorium. You have been in school all day and talked to every one of us. *Now can you end this crap and just come to the rehearsal?*"

"I have to go to work, Brianna," Harrison said. "Weren't you listening? I cannot do the show. I cannot stay after school."

"Right," Brianna said. "Right. You said that a hundred times. Sorry I asked. Have a good time at Kostas Korner. Give Guillermo a kiss for me."

She spun away from him and headed downstairs toward the auditorium. She could have kicked herself. She had promised herself she wouldn't beg. She had told everyone else not to.

Casey was waiting at the bottom of the stairs. "What did he say?" she asked.

"I feel defiled," she said. "I actually asked him to come to the rehearsal. He said no, of course."

"Well, *I'm* glad you asked," Casey said with a sigh.

Reese and Charles were just inside the auditorium, looking at some notes on a script, while Dashiell conferred with Ripley at the back. "Danny's in a lot of dance numbers," Reese said. "This is going to be a lot of work."

"Plus it's so sad," Charles added. "We will miss our Prince Harrison . . . "

"Brianna!" cried Dashiell, rushing over. "Did you talk to him? I thought I detected in his facial expression a hidden desire to return."

"She had no luck," Reese said, kicking her leg over her head and stretching it against the wall. "I'll be happy to work on him, but I can't promise anything."

"I'll get a 'Do Not Disturb' sign for the Green Room," Charles offered.

"Don't bother, guys," Brianna said. "Leave him alone. He's history, at least for this musical."

"Who are we going to cast?" Reese asked. "Devon

Roper? We asked him to be one of the Burger Palace Boys and he refused. Are we supposed to reward him for turning us down? And do you think I'm going to let myself be alone in the Green Room with him?"

"It'll continue a tradition," Brianna said.

Reese arched backward. "I think I was just insulted."

"How about Barry?" Charles asked.

"Vocally appropriate," said Dashiell, "but then who would play Kenickie? I don't see this working without Harrison."

Brianna wanted to scream. They were talking themselves into a circle of wishful thinking. "Look, we're the Drama Club," she said. "We're in goddamn Ridgeport. If we can't find a goddamn Danny Zuko, no one can. This is not *Hamlet*. Wake up, guys. What's wrong with you? *What's wrong with all of you? Why are you being so negative?*"

Reese, Charles, and Dashiell all stared at her, speechless.

"Couldn't help overhearing," Chip Duggan said, bouncing over. "I have the lines nearly memorized. I have a photographic—"

"*Go away, Chip!*" Brianna snapped.

"You're right," he shot back. "Not the right type. Never mind."

As he scurried away, Brianna took a deep breath and closed her eyes. Against all the staring faces, the talking, the hyperventilating.

"That's it, sugar," Charles said soothingly. "It's been a very bad, no-good, horrible day. Count to thirty-seven slowly. And then when you open your eyes, *poof*, it will all be seashells and ice cream again."

Brianna's forehead hurt. Her eyes felt as if they were lined with very fine sandpaper. They weren't getting it. They weren't getting what this really meant. Like this was all a game. Like it was crazy to have professional standards.

Like I'm some kind of crazy person.

Well, someone had to make a smart decision. To think clearly.

She opened her eyes. They were all staring at her. Casey had been staring at her a lot lately. Judging her. Charles, too.

Well, to hell with all of them.

Through the open door to the hallway, she spotted a volleyball skittering across the floor, chased by two guys shoving each other.

And the solution came to her. It wasn't foolproof, but it could work. She could make it work.

"We can do this play," she said. "And it will be even better without Harrison. I know how."

"Do tell," Charles said, "because I am about to schedule an emergency session with Dr. Eustis Fink the Useless Shrink. For all of us."

Brianna stepped into the aisle. "Okay. You can follow me if you want. If not, I will see you later with a Danny."

24

"WANT SOME?" SAID KYLE WITH A GRIN, OFFERING Brianna his half-eaten Dove Bar.

"That's the wrong answer. We asked you a question. You may not answer us with a question. Especially a dumb one." As Brianna sat next to Kyle in the hallway near his locker, Casey, Charles, Reese, and Dashiell knelt around them. "Now watch my lips and do this . . . *yyyes*, Brianna, yes, I can play Danny Zuko."

Kyle burst out laughing. "Right. In my spare time. Sorry, guys, I can't. I have this commitment. Practices, meets—"

"Think of your future," Charles piped up. "Acting is useful in so many ways. Throwing sticks is old school. So hunter-gatherer."

"It's a javelin," Kyle said. "And it's my event. I can't let the team down."

"We're your team, too," Reese said, sidling close to him.

"You were born to play this role, Kyle," Dashiell added. "And as student director, I have techniques that will save you time by accelerating memorization and blocking, including a virtual 3-D scene-by-scene digital schematic."

"Don't scare him out of it," Charles warned.

Kyle took another bite and rubbed his forehead. "Look, guys. Even if I *could* do it? It's Harrison's part. I would feel funny taking it."

If I could. That was promising. Brianna leaned in. "You would feel better letting someone else do it? Someone *less* than the best? Because that's what will happen. Put yourself in Harrison's head. Can you imagine him thinking, *Hey, cool, someone mediocre is taking over my part?* Don't you think he would want *you* to do it—his old *Godspell* partner?"

Casey slid her clipboard toward him. "Here are the remaining rehearsals, right up to the weekend of performances. We have seven weeks left, plenty of time."

"Whoa! Whoa, easy, guys!" Kyle said. "I said *no.*"

"We are being hypothetical," Dashiell said. "Now, hypothetically, say we could arrange something—like, you could come late to rehearsals to allow for track. How much of a hypothetical conflict would it be?"

"Uh . . . big?" Kyle glanced at Casey's schedule. "You've got three weekday rehearsals and one or two on the weekend. And track..." He shook his head, started to get up, then paused. "Actually, I'm not doing a team event, so I don't have to be at track practices the *whole* time, but— "

"So then you *could* rehearse!" Dashiell burst out. "Hypothetically."

"Yeah, and Coach Emmons would kill me," Kyle replied.

"*Ask* him," Brianna said.

Kyle laughed. "Easy for you to say."

Brianna bolted to her feet. "I'll ask him. I'm not scared."

"I'm not *scared* either," Kyle said, tossing the Dove Bar wrapper and stick clear across the hallway in an arc and directly into the trash. "Two points! Look, I'm twice the size of Emmons. But I can't do it to him. It would be selfish. Nobody pulls that kind of stunt."

"Okay, your choice," Brianna said, turning back with a sigh. "You go ahead and throw the javelin. We'll get Devon to do Danny."

"Devon?" Kyle said. "You're going to let *that guy* play the lead?"

"He's a good singer," Casey said.

"He's a prick," Kyle replied.

Brianna turned. "Well, yeah. But we'll deal. Don't forget to come see him act with all your old friends. Come on, everybody!"

"Brianna?" Casey whispered.

Brianna grabbed her and Reese by the sleeves. "Come on. You, too, Charles. Dashiell?"

In a moment they were in the lobby.

"We haven't cast Devon!" Charles said.

"I know," Brianna replied.

"I'll work on him," Reese said with a sly smile. "I have ways with Kyle."

Brianna moved to a side hallway, which had a window looking out onto the field. "I don't think you're going to need to."

She put her finger to her lips and gestured out the window. It was a warm day for February, maybe fifty degrees, and a gym class was outside in sweats, running laps. Coach Emmons stood by the fence, egging them on.

Brianna rested her hands on the door. They were shaking. Which was annoying. They had been shaking a lot lately. For no reason.

"Um, what are we doing here?" Reese asked.

"Just be patient . . . " Brianna said.

Now Kyle was jogging across the field, in his sweats. He headed straight for the coach.

They all leaned close to the window.

"Well, now, this situation is pregnant with possibility," Dashiell said. "Do you suppose he *is* asking?"

Brianna shrugged. "Kyle has an ego. He loves applause. He loves it when people need him."

As Kyle began talking, Coach Emmons nodded curiously. Brianna couldn't hear what he was saying, but the coach's face quickly changed. And he did not look happy.

He said a few words to Kyle. Intensely. Sports-coachishly.

A nod, a glance at a clipboard, and Kyle was running, back onto the track.

"Do you think he asked?" Casey said.

"Nahhh," Charles replied. "That was guy talk. Probably discussing the length of their javelins."

Reese laughed. "That's girl talk."

"Well," Dashiell said, "we made a valiant attempt. Thank you for your persistence, Brianna."

Brianna exhaled and turned away. Together they walked quietly across the lobby and down the hall to the auditorium.

"What's Devon's cell number?" Casey asked.

"Five-one-six . . . " Brianna stopped herself. Not a smart idea to let everyone know *she* knew. "I think I have it written down somewhere. From the first audition."

As she reached for the auditorium door, an arm reached around her and pulled it open. "After you."

It was Kyle. With a big dimply grin.

"Wait—you were just outside," Reese said.

"I move fast," Kyle replied. "I just wanted to tell you, I talked to Coach. About the show."

"We saw," Charles said. "Oops. There goes our little secret."

"So he tells me he tried to be an actor, right out of college," Kyle said. "He was on three soap operas and two TV shows. In all of them, he was a cop. No lines. Said it was the most boring way to make a living. So he left the business."

"Just our luck, Coach Emmons is a failed actor," Brianna said. "So he told you to come here and yell at us?"

"He was there at closing night of *Godspell*," Kyle went on. "He said he went home totally pissed off. He didn't think I would ever do anything athletic ever again. So he was amazed and happy when I tried out for track."

"Everybody loves Kyle," Reese said.

"He said *Godspell* was the best show he ever saw in eighteen years at Ridgeport. But *Grease* is his favorite musical of all time. So you know what he says to me?" Kyle grinned. "He says, 'If you pass this up, you're crazier than I thought.'"

"Whaaaat?" Reese said.

Brianna raised an eyebrow. Kyle was sneaky. He had a twisted sense of humor for someone so straight and jockish. There might be a punch line here she wouldn't like.

"He said, and I quote"—Kyle pitched his voice to sound like Coach Emmons and almost nailed it—" 'I'll keep you on the javelin. We'll work it out. But if you don't get your butt to the next Drama Club rehearsal, you're doing the shot put *and* cross-country.' "

Reese let out a shriek and jumped on him. Dashiell let out a cheer and started dancing. Charles, despite having never showed signs of religion, did the sign of the cross. And Casey beamed at Brianna.

Brianna's hands were shaking big-time now.

But she didn't care.

25

Saturday, February 2, 1:13 A.M.

dramakween: harrison?

dramakween: ru there?

dramakween: u haven't left for chicago yet, right? that's tmw . . .

dramakween: im bored. im scared. i don't know why, i just feel crappy. also I want to talk about kyle, I need your advice cuz he could be better. i wish you were at rehearsals. i feel like i suck at being rizzo too.

dramakween: pleeeeeeeez answer

dramakween: im not mad at you.

dramakween: well not much.

dramakween: i wont bite ☺

dramakween: wtf????????????????

dramakween: was it something i ate?

dramakween: i know ur there!!!

dramakween: DAMMIT HARRISON ANSWER ME!!!!!!!!!!!!!!!!!!!!!!

pedl2METL: yo

pedl2METL: sup?

pedl2METL: u there?

pedl2METL: its late

pedl2METL: i can come over if ur not feeling good.

dramakween: im fine, devon. working.

pedl2METL: b right over?

dramakween: no. im tired & i have too much work to do

pedl2METL: that's usually when u DO want to see me. lol

pedl2METL: well if u change yr mind let me know i need my beauty sleep too

dramakween has signed off.

"No no no—*upstage* at the top of the number!" Dashiell called out. "Upstage left! And sing out!"

Kyle pointed his thumb toward the back of the stage. "Upstage is that way? I keep getting confused."

"Yes!"

"And stage left is *my* left?" he asked, looking toward the side of the stage that was totally unlit. "The dark part?"

Casey buried her head in her hands. The lighting had been screwed up all week. It was a major annoyance, but it had to be put in perspective. It was only Thursday, February 7. Still six weeks to go.

The big news was Kyle. His presence had picked up everyone's spirits. At least for a couple of rehearsals.

"*Um, we prefer lights?*" Charles shouted from backstage.

"RIPLEEEEEY!" Mr. Levin cried out.

"I'll troubleshoot," Dashiell said, dropping his clipboard and heading up the aisle. "Casey, can you coach Kyle? I will have a little confabulation with my feckless successor in the projection room."

"Sure," Casey said.

As she jumped onstage, the set was suddenly bathed in red. "That's festive," Charles said.

"Kyle, you're doing great," Casey said. "But—"

"There's a lot of dancing," Kyle replied.

"You can't stop singing, though," Casey said. "You're going to have a body mike. People will notice."

"I suck at dancing," Kyle said.

"You look great," Casey insisted. "You danced really well in *Godspell*."

"That was just jumping around. This is counting. And doing the same stuff everyone else is doing. It's different."

Reese rushed in from stage left. "I can rechoreograph it. I did the choreo with Harrison in mind. Here, do this with me."

She held his hand and began teaching a new step.

"Everyone besides Reese and Kyle, take a break!" Casey announced, looking at her schedule. "In five minutes, we're doing Act One, Scene Four—Marty's bedroom, leading into 'Freddy, My Love'! I need Marty, Frenchy, Jan, and Rizzo!"

She glanced out into the house for the four actresses. "Charles? Have you seen Brianna?"

Charles shook his head. "With the current lighting dilemma, I haven't seen much of anything."

"Rizzo?" Casey called out. "*Brianna?*"

Chip Duggan came in through the side door and raced to the stage. "Um, she's indisposed, I think," he said softly, almost in a whisper. His face was red.

"What do you mean?" Casey whispered back.

"I was in the men's room, experimenting with hairstyles," Chip said, "when the door opened. I wouldn't have paid much attention, but it was a she, and she was running."

"Brianna?" Casey asked.

Chip nodded. "Correct. She went straight into a stall and shut it. I believe she was vomiting, but I can't be sure because she was flushing repeatedly."

Vomiting.

"Oh God . . . " Casey murmured. She eyed Mr. Levin, who was deep in conversation with Corbin about something. It was not necessary to bring Mr. Levin into this.

"There is a strain of flu going around," Chip said. "My father is a doctor and makes sure I receive an annual inoculation—so you don't need to worry about me—but he says that this year—"

"Chip," Casey said, "can you run up to Dashiell in the projection booth and tell him he needs to come back right now?"

"Of course!" Chip said, bounding away.

Kyle, striking a pose onstage, called out, "Case, I got it . . . I think!"

"Great," Casey said. "Be right back. Talk to Dashiell when he gets here."

She ran out the side door, into the hallway, and straight to the men's room. She nearly knocked over Ethan, who was just emerging.

"Eek," he said.

"Is Brianna in there?" Casey asked.

"Not that I could see," Ethan said. "Of course, I wouldn't be surprised. She's been after my body for months."

Casey barged in and let the door swing closed behind her. The room appeared empty. All of the stalls were open except the last. "Brianna?" Casey called out.

She knocked on the stall door. "Brianna? Are you there?"

"Just a minute," came Brianna's voice, sounding a little startled.

The toilet flushed, and Brianna emerged a moment later. "It's closer to the auditorium, which is why I came in here—the convenience—but it isn't as nice," she said. "Why are *you* here?"

"I heard you were sick."

"Aren't *you*? It smells terrible in here. Boys are pigs."

"Someone saw you come in. He kept hearing the toilet flush."

"You mean Chip? I was trying to get rid of him. I think he wanted to peek under the stall. I figured the flushing would drive him a little crazy and he would go away."

Brianna quickly washed her hands. "Is the break over yet?"

"Yeah," Casey replied. "See you out there."

"Hurry," Brianna said.

Casey waited for Brianna to leave. She had to collect herself.

It was pretty obvious that Chip had called it. It wasn't that difficult for Casey to tell. Brianna could hide a lot with her confidence, her sense of humor, her star power. But she couldn't hide this.

It wasn't the flu, Casey knew. It was something no one suspected. Everyone else saw only Brianna the Perfect. Brianna the Star.

Casey held on to the wall, steadying herself. She had to do something. Stars could burn out. And this one was on its way.

26

IT WAS WORKING OUT JUST FINE, HARRISON told himself.

The funeral in Chicago had been sad but short. It was interesting to meet cousins he had never met before.

It had been painful to leave the DC. But it could have been worse. It could have been some Sondheim show, like *Into the Woods* or *Sweeney Todd*, instead of *Grease*.

The Drama Club was going to do all right without him. It was Thursday and Kyle had been rehearsing for nearly a week. He had been born to play Danny. It was totally right.

In a way, Harrison thought, he had done the most unselfish thing of all.

He yanked the steering wheel to the right and almost mounted the curb. Whoops. It was nice that Craig let him use his beat-up old Taurus.

Gliding past his own house in the darkness of night, knowing no one could see him through the tinted windows, he felt like a stranger cruising the neighborhood. Suddenly the house looked funny to him—the fakeness of the aluminum siding, the light blue dormers, the Christmas lights still strung around the porch in February, the tacky fluorescent Frosty the Snowman on the door holding the Greek flag.

Harrison wondered what would happen if his dad came outside. What would they say? They hadn't spoken in days. Not on the plane, not at the funeral service. Even at the diner, Dad had avoided him. Mom had done all the talking.

He drove onto Sunrise and made the long ride into the Heights. Turning up Oak Drive, he parked across the street from number 45, the Glasers' house. The lights were on. Through the bay windows he could see some movement— Siobhan and Colter scurrying around. Brianna's windows were dark. Maybe rehearsal had run late.

She had been really cold to him for the last few days. Everyone else seemed to understand . . .

Flipping open his cell, he called Brianna.

Voice mail.

"Call me," he said. "I'm around."

He was about to put the phone away but thought better of it. Instead he tapped out the number again and this time left a text message.

```
HEY ITS ME WANNA GET SOME PIZZA?
```

He pressed Send and put the phone away.

It beeped a moment later. He sat up and looked at the screen:

```
GO F YOURSELF
```

27

BRIANNA PUT THE PHONE AWAY.

As she walked onto the beach, she didn't feel the cold. She wasn't even affected by the darkness. In the distance she could hear waves lapping against the jetty. Shells crunched beneath her feet and soon she felt seawater ooze between her toes.

It felt so good to be away. Away from all of them. Casey, Charles, Reese, Dashiell, Kyle, Harrison.

She was tired of worrying about other people. She needed to think about herself.

Learning the role of Rizzo had been unbelievably hard. Her main song—"There Are Worse Things I Could Do"—was not in Brianna's range by a long shot. At least not lately. Dashiell wasn't giving her any directions either. He was concentrating on Kyle.

That was part of the problem. Kyle—her great casting idea—well, with Harrison at his side in *Godspell*, Kyle had been great. Without him, not so good. There was no Jesus without John, she guessed. No rebirth without a baptism.

She stopped near the old wooden sign. DANGEROUS: KEEP OFF THE JETTY.

This was where Kyle had thrown the umbrella.

She climbed the rocks. They were slippery. The surf slapped lazily at her feet as she walked, farther and farther. It was so beautiful out here, so peaceful.

A ship's light blinked in the distance. Around her the sea stretched black and vast, merging with the sky.

Brianna could see how Kyle liked being here in the winter. The air entered you in a different way. You could feel it like a drink. It tickled whatever was rotting inside.

She took a deep breath and turned. A spray of seawater caught her left calf, and she nearly slipped into a crevice. It really wasn't safe up here.

Carefully she walked back and jumped onto the sand. She walked quickly back, past the sign.

This was where he had pulled his Polar Bear stunt.

Thinking about it, she grinned. He had been so exhilarated. Like a kid. Like he had been shot through with new life.

It had been freezing that night.

She pulled off her sweater. It wasn't so bad, not nearly as arctic as that night with Kyle.

She took off her shirt, felt the wind against her bare skin. She wasn't as cold as she thought she would be. It felt invigorating. Bracing.

Her tank top came off next, then her jeans. One by one, she peeled off every piece of clothing she was wearing, save her underwear, and set it all in a neat pile.

The surf rushed the shore. She felt freedom. Happiness. She stretched out her arms, embracing the ocean.

It was wonderful.

Liberating.

She laughed, her voice brittle and soft in the wintry air. The wind whipped every pore of her skin. Lifting her.

And then she began to run, faster and faster.

To the sea.

Part 3
All Alone

Thursday, February 7

28

"YOU'RE SURE SHE WAS PUKING," CHARLES SAID, driving into the parking lot of Jones Beach West End One.

"Yes," Casey said. "And she knew Devon Roper's phone number, I could tell. He's been giving her drugs. Or somebody has. I saw them on her desk the other night. With a strange note. 'From a secret admirer.' I wish I had said something. I wish I hadn't taken so long."

"This is creepy," Charles said. "We're chasing her down like the junior FBI."

"We were heading to her house to talk, just as she drove away," Casey reminded him. "What else were we supposed to do? And where can she have gone? We've checked almost every parking lot."

She squinted into the distance, scanning the periphery of the lot. Just outside the pool of light from a street lamp, a minivan sat at an odd angle.

Charles saw it too. "That's hers!" he said.

He pulled into a spot and they both climbed out.

Casey ran to the boardwalk and looked out over the sand. There wasn't much light, but she could spot a dark figure by the water. "Look, there she is."

"That *can't* be her," Charles said. "That person is going into the water. La Glaser would *not*—"

Casey broke into a run. "COME ON!"

She couldn't quite believe what she was seeing. Brianna was running toward the water *in her underwear.*

No, not even that.

"OH MY GOD! BRIANNA! *BRIANNAAAAA!*" Casey shouted.

Brianna was in the water now. Stepping high, being battered by waves that broke at her knees. She was making a sound, too. Something like a moan.

Casey ran after her, into the surf. Her footing gave way and she fell. The shock of the water made her gasp. Water slapped against her face. The darkness turned white and she felt her heart lurch.

Behind her, Charles was screaming. *"Casey, what are you doing?"*

Casey struggled to her feet. Charles's arm hooked under hers, pulling her upward. They both charged deeper in. The cold stung.

"Brianna, where are you?" Charles shouted.

She was gone. Casey couldn't see her.

"GEEEEAAHHHH!"

There. Ten feet in front of them, her head broke out of the water. Brianna was flailing. *"Oh God!"* she screamed.

Charles dived. He came up next to Brianna and grabbed her hand. "Help!" he cried out.

Casey fought to keep conscious. She couldn't feel her own hands and feet. She sank back into the water and pushed herself forward. Somehow that was better, but not by much.

"Put her arm arr-r-r-round your sh-sh-sh—" Charles stammered.

Casey willed her own arm to move. She was shaking. It took three tries. "Got her!"

A swell of water lifted them up, off the sandy bottom. Sideways and backward.

"K-k-kuh—" Charles gasped.

Kick. Casey moved her legs. Scissoring against the current.

It wasn't working. They were getting farther away from the shore.

As Casey's feet reached bottom again, another wave bounced them high. Casey went under and emerged, coughing. Her lungs felt as if they had been flayed open. She coughed, trying to keep her head up. Seawater came through her mouth and nose. She struggled to hold tight to Brianna.

"Are y-y-y-you ok-k-kay?" Charles shouted.

"NO!" Casey replied.

Brianna was going limp. The current was tugging them back and to the right. Out to sea.

A spit of rocks was the only thing between them and the ocean.

The jetty.

Casey moved sideways, with Charles. They were heading past the tip of the jetty, out to sea. She began fighting the current again, but this time just trying to change the path slightly . . .

She could feel Charles pulling hard. He was a strong swimmer. She kicked . . . kicked . . .

Her breath was starting to give out, her eyes blurring. Casey felt herself letting go of Brianna.

She lost her. She lost contact with everything. And she was falling, being enveloped by darkness.

Sinking.

Alone.

29

WHEN HIS CELL PHONE RANG, HARRISON SPRANG up in bed. His head hit the ceiling with a loud thump.

"Is that yours? The phone?" Craig asked.

"Yup." Harrison fumbled in the pocket of his pants, which were hung over the edge of the bed. He wasn't used to sleeping in a strange room, and the last thing he wanted was to wake the Weigels.

"Hello?" he whispered into the phone.

"Harr . . . on? . . . you . . . ake?"

The voice was breaking up, but it sounded like Charles. "Charles? Is that you?"

" . . . ear . . . ee?"

"I can't hear you," Harrison said.

"IS THAT BETTER?" Charles said. "IT'S SO

FRIGGIN' WINDY! HARRISON, IF YOU CAN HEAR ME, CAN YOU COME TO JONES BEACH?"

"Jones Beach? *Now?*"

"BRING TOWELS AND BLANKETS. LOTS OF TOWELS AND BLANKETS. AND CLOTHES, TOO! T-SHIRTS, JEANS, SOCKS, COATS!!"

"Is this some kind of joke—?"

"JUST COME, HARRISON! WEST END ONE! THIS IS LIFE OR DEATH!"

He was there in minutes. The cars were easy to spot. They were the only ones in the lot. One of them was the Glasers' minivan. The motor was running.

A silhouette leaped out and waved at him. Charles.

"Over h-h-here!" he called. "T-took you long enough. Do y-y-you have blankets and t-t-towels?"

Harrison sped over and parked. The rear of the minivan was open and two people were lying inside. Charles was soaking wet and shivering. "What the hell happened?" Harrison said.

"What d-d-does it look like?" Charles snapped. "We w-w-ent for a swim!"

Racing around to the back of the car, Harrison pulled open the trunk. He handed Charles the pile of thick linens that Craig had helped him find.

Together he and Charles ran to the back of the minivan. He could hear Brianna shivering and sobbing. "Harrison . . . " she moaned.

Harrison climbed in and wrapped Brianna in a blanket. "This will warm you up," he told her. He had never seen her look so lost. "It's okay," he found himself murmuring. "You're going to be all right."

"Shut the door, the heat's escaping," Charles said, wrapping Casey in another blanket. "I've got it turned as high as it goes. I'm going to change. Thanks for bringing clothes."

As Charles scrambled into the front seat, Harrison piled as many layers of clothing as he could on each girl.

Casey stirred, opening her eyes briefly. "Thank . . . you . . . " she mumbled.

"It's my fault," Brianna said. "I did it. It's all my fault."

"What did you do, Brianna?" Harrison said. "What is going on?"

"I thought it would . . . I wanted to clear my . . . to be clear . . . to . . ."

Charles came back, wiping his hair with a towel. He was wearing Craig's striped button-down shirt, which was way too tight, and a pair of jeans that did not close at the waist. "Brianna decided to be a Polar Bear," he said. "Don't ask. We'll find out later, I suppose. We went in to get her. Casey swallowed water."

"So . . . *you* saved them?"

Charles managed a smile. "Lifeguard certificate, Camp Sangamon—not bad for a *maláka*," he said. "Now come on, we have to get them home. I'll call Casey's mom. She's a nurse. She'll know what to do. Will you drive? I can't, not right now. We can come back and get the other cars later."

"Fine. Take a beach towel. It'll warm you up."

Charles grabbed it and wrapped it around his body. "And more importantly," he said, "it will hide this hideous outfit from an inquiring public."

30

"BRIANNA?"

It was her mom's voice. Brianna blinked, allowing her bedroom to come into focus.

Mom sat in the desk chair, Dad in the armchair. Both were leaning toward her. Her mom ran her fingers through Brianna's hair and sniffed softly. "Everything's all right, baby," she said. "Don't worry."

Her dad opened his mouth to say something but no words came out. Behind his thick professor's beard and perfectly kept haircut, he had always seemed ageless to Brianna. But today he looked fragile and old.

Not *today*. Tonight. On her night table, her alarm clock showed 11:49.

"Hi," Brianna said. "What—how did I get here?"

"Harrison," her dad replied. "Charles and Casey are

downstairs in the living room, sipping hot chocolate by the fireplace. They're fine. Their parents are down there, too. Harrison's right here."

She felt a little pinch on her foot. Harrison was sitting at the bottom of the bed, smiling down at her. "Charles and Casey found you at the beach," he said. "They said you were in the water."

Brianna closed her eyes.

The water.

The Polar Bear Club.

Her head was throbbing. "I—I wasn't feeling good," she said. "I thought . . . if I went to the beach I'd feel . . . I don't know . . . "

Her mom gently took her hand. "Was anyone else there, honey? Was Kyle with you?"

"You were—you didn't have—" Harrison stammered. "They said your clothes were on the shore. So maybe . . ."

Brianna flinched. Yes, she remembered now. The air, the jetty, the ocean . . . the feeling that she just *had* to go in. As she thought about it now, it seemed unreal. Like she'd become another person.

And now they were staring at her. Alarmed. As if . . .

The clothes . . . Kyle . . .

"Oh my God," she said. "You think . . . you think something like *that* happened? *Kyle wasn't there.* I was alone. I went into the water by myself."

Her mom's lips were quivering. "So . . . you . . . you *planned* to do this . . . ?"

"Why, sweetie?" her dad added. "Is it something we did?"

Brianna closed her eyes. Nobody was getting it.

Which was understandable. It wasn't making sense to her either.

"It wasn't a suicide attempt," she said wearily. "It was . . . the opposite. Some other kind of attempt—I don't know what it was." She took a deep breath. "I don't know why I did it. I just did it. I didn't mean to harm myself. I just wanted to dip in and then dip out. I thought it would make me feel better."

"But . . . there are all those no-swimming signs," her dad said.

"I know, I know. I'm sorry. I was an idiot." Brianna felt tears pushing their way up. "It's all my fault . . ."

"No, no, sweetie, it's no one's fault," her mom assured her.

"I wrecked everyone's lives," Brianna said. "Charles, Casey, Harrison . . . my best friends!"

"Everyone's fine," her dad replied. "Just think about you."

"Me? Do I have to? Oh God, I have so much to do, Dad . . . how am I going to . . . *why did I do this to myself* . . . to everybody . . . ?"

"Shhh, shhh," her mom said. "We're going to figure this out . . . "

"We're going to get you help—" said her dad.

He was interrupted by the ringing of the front doorbell. Hopping up from the seat, he quickly left the room and went to answer it.

A moment later, a familiar face peered into the room, and under it and a foil-covered plate of God-knew-what.

"You like the baklava?" asked Mr. Michaels with a great big warm smile.

Harrison smiled back at him.

And Brianna began to cry.

31

YaLeBiRd: *omg bri is this some kind of a joke?*
dramakween: nope
YaLeBiRd: *substance abuse?????*
dramakween: cue violins
dramakween: im like an after-school special
YaLeBiRd: *god this isnt funny i miss u & i wish i could b there!!!!!*
YaLeBiRd: *ok y did u go in the water?????*
dramakween: strung out i guess. dr. fink sez i was being grandiose
dramakween: but we knew that lol
dramakween: (& my parents pay him . . .)
dramakween: anyway i remembered kyle did it. i

thought it would be cool. it was weird, i didnt really think about it i just kinda did it?

YaLeBiRd: *are u doing like a 12-step thing*

dramakween: mm. yup.

dramakween: 12 steps from the kitchen to my bedroom.

dramakween: mom & dad r making me take a couple of days off. to chill. all the teachers r cool with it.

YaLeBiRd: *ok, im coming to visit!*

dramakween: nice. bring chocolate.

dramakween: & a thick letter from yale admissions addressed to brianna glaser

"It's not your fault, Harrison," Brianna said, blowing gently across a cup of tea in a paper cup he had brought from the diner, labeled GOD BLESS AMERICA AND DON'T FORGET THE COFFEE!

She felt better. Well rested. She'd had more phone calls and cards and well-wishes than she'd had for her bat mitzvah.

Missing school on Friday had made her nervous. Until she dug into a trashy vampire novel that Charles had sent over and didn't stop reading until she had finished.

"I didn't help things by running from the DC," Harrison said, hanging his head and looking tortured. "I added to your troubles. I owe you. I owe you big-time."

Brianna leaned forward and wrapped her arms around him. "I don't know why I'm comforting you," she said.

He squeezed her back, hard. "That thing I said? About you being a mistake? I didn't mean it, Brianna."

Brianna smiled. "Nice to know," she said.

"People change . . ."

His words hung in the air.

She felt it. Things had changed. But at the moment, she didn't feel a need to know why. Or how. She was happy to let things take their course. "Well, maybe we can talk about it," Brianna said, "after I feel better. Look, Harrison. Staying in bed like this? Saying 'screw you' to school for a couple of days? It's the bomb. I recommend it. I've been sleeping. I'd gotten to the point where I forgot what that was like."

"So . . . you're not worried?" Harrison asked. "I know you. You worry about crap like this. Being absent and missing work."

Brianna shrugged. "I guess I am. But I'm getting the work and focusing on doing it instead of freaking out. It's just that I prefer being sane. And I like it when people bring me tea in a paper coffee cup."

"I keep telling Dad to change that slogan."

"Harrison?" Brianna reached out and pulled his face toward her. "Tell me the truth. What's up with you and your dad? Are you really going to live with the Weigels for that whole forty days, just to spite him?"

"Just because we had baklava together doesn't mean we're all better."

Brianna sipped at her tea and thought a moment. "I wish you could see the rehearsals, Harrison. Kyle needs help. He's not doing so great as Danny. In fact, he's kind of screwing up."

Harrison raised an eyebrow. "Uh, Brianna, lies will not get me to come to rehearsals."

"He looks uncomfortable, like he doesn't want to do it." Brianna shrugged. "I think he's like Samson. And you're the hair."

"Ouch," Harrison said.

"Are you *sure* you can't do the role? I think Kyle would understand."

"Nope, but I'll talk to him, during the school day."

"You are so stubborn."

"My hands are tied, Brianna. I didn't choose this."

"What about now?" Brianna said.

Harrison laughed. "I have to go back to the Weigels' now. I have homework, too."

"You never do homework on Saturdays. Look, this is important. And I am the acting president of the Drama Club, so I'm pulling rank. Call Kyle. Invite him to the Weigels' and start coaching him. Now."

"Since when are you acting president?"

"You can't stay after school. That disqualifies you! And don't change the subject, Harrison. You are being stubborn."

"Some things never change." Harrison stood up and scooted out the door. "Bye, Bri. Glad you're feeling better."

She heard him clomp down the stairs. She had the urge to throw something after him. Which was comforting, in a way. Maybe a sign that things were getting back to normal.

Then his voice filtered up from downstairs. "Yeah, hey, Kyle, it's Harrison. Can you come over? Craig Weigel's. We can work on the show . . . "

Brianna smiled and sipped her tea.

* * *

A few hours later, Kyle was at the Weigels'.

"Think *slacker*," Harrison said as they ran through a scene in the basement. "You're a little stupid, and you don't feel like improving."

Kyle let his shoulders droop. His eyes suddenly got dull. "Like this?"

"Perfect! And when you do the choreo to 'Summer Lovin',' think *into the floor*. Like you're stomping on cockroaches, okay? Right now your body movements are a little too hip-hop. Too bouncy. The center of gravity is too high."

"Uh-huh . . . " Kyle began snapping his fingers and shaking his legs to an imaginary beat. "Yo. Dude."

"Not *yo* and not *dude*. It's the fifties. It's like, *hey*, and *daddy-o*."

"Hey . . . " *Snap-snap-snap.* "Daddy-o . . . "

Harrison looked away so he wouldn't crack up. "Let's sing it. I'll do Sandy's part."

He flipped on the CD player, and the Broadway cast album of *Grease* echoed through the basement. "One, two, *ready*, *go!*"

Tentatively Kyle sang the opening line to "Summer Lovin'."

At the top of his lungs, Harrison answered back Sandy's part, in a wailing falsetto.

"Dude, you are hot," Kyle said.

"Come and get me, Danny boy," Harrison responded with a wink.

Together they blasted their way through the song, bumping hips and roughing out the dance steps.

After the last line, Kyle fell to the floor. "WOO-HOOOOO! What a friggin' couple! Man, I wanna marry you!"

Harrison flicked off the CD player. "You're not bad. Or tentative. Or confused. I don't care what they say."

"*Who* says?" Kyle asked.

"Brianna. She said you were making mistakes and not looking confident."

"Oh. That. Yeah. I just needed the right coach, that's all."

"Well, as Charles would say, just leave the money in my locker on the way out."

"No way. I'm broke."

"Then I'll have to sue," Harrison replied.

"Does this mean," Kyle said solemnly, "we can't get married?"

32

"SUMMER LOVIN' IS IN THE AIR. GOOD MORNIN',
guys and gals, it's Monday, February eleventh, only five
weeks and five days till opening, and yes, it's GREASE
DAY! This is Dreamy Dash, doing the do on here on
WRHS, the official station of Ridgep— I mean, Rydell
High. Are you wearing your Grease clothing? Lemme hear
you say YEAH!"

Cascy cocked her ear to the hallway. She heard a blast
of "YEAH," but it was mostly from Drama Club members
in the lobby.

The Ridgeport "radio station" was a small room with
a soundproof booth hooked up to the school PA system.
From behind the booth's glass window, Dashiell looked at
her expectantly.

She gave him a thumbs-up.

"*So remember, dig up some scratch, and get your student tix at the principal's office or from any Drama Club officer! Be there or be square!*"

"He's trying," Charles said.

"Doo-wop-WOP . . . doo-wop-a-diddy-diddy . . . "

At the sound of a cappella singing, Casey ducked into the hallway.

Against the Wall of Fame, a group of guys dressed in leather jackets, white T-shirts, and cuffed jeans were snapping their fingers and singing. Corbin and Ethan, two Drama Club regulars, were among them—they were the Vanderdonks, the school's male a cappella group.

Mr. Ippolito, the school custodian, was in front. He had a jeans jacket over his janitorial clothes. He had dyed his hair jet-black and slicked it back into a ducktail. "Ohhh . . . ohhh, my baby . . . " he wailed, taking the solo.

Casey cracked up. "He's *good!*"

"If you don't mind that he's in the wrong key," Charles said.

"OOHHHHH, SALVATORRRRRE!" shrieked Ms. Hecksher, the principal, emerging from her office and running toward Mr. Ippolito. She was decked out in bobby socks, white bucks, a pleated skirt, and a cardigan over a white shirt. She wore a string of pearls and her hair was teased into a bouffant.

Charles staggered backward. "Oh, dear God, will someone take a photo for future blackmail."

"Mr. Ippolito's name is *Salvatore?*" Casey said.

"Doo-wop-wop . . . doo-wop-a-diddy-diddy . . ."

Mr. Ippolito pulled Ms. Hecksher into a clumsy

jitterbug. Another couple started up, too, and another, until the lobby was jumping.

"Nifty!" cried Chip, adjusting his glasses. "Keen!"

He smiled at Casey. She smiled back. She had been working with him on Eugene. He was really getting the hang of it.

After school that day, Harrison slipped into the auditorium and sat in the shadowed corner of the back row, one of the only places the houselights didn't reach. He wasn't supposed to be there. The forty days was nowhere near over. But his shift was starting a little late. He figured it wouldn't hurt just to peek.

The Pink Ladies had just sung "Freddy My Love," and Reese was calling for the scene leading into "I'm All Alone at the Drive-In Movie."

It was Harrison's favorite scene.

Shara and Kyle were in a spotlight, sitting in the hot rod and pretending to watch an outdoor movie. Kyle gave a huge exaggerated yawn, stretching his arms out, and . . . THUMP . . . his arm plopped onto Shara's shoulder.

Sitting in the first two rows, the cast members broke out laughing.

Kyle was funny. Harrison knew how hard that was. Harder than people thought. It was one of those things— you either had it or you didn't.

Harrison watched in amazement, trying to hold back his envy. The attempted hookup . . . the kiss . . .

He was nailing it all. Kyle gave great Bumbling-Egotistical-Fool.

Shara was angrily leaving the car now. Slamming the

car door . . . the gag was, it would hit him right in the . . .

No. All wrong.

She was supposed to slam the door on his privates. Harrison had worked hard on that. But the bit was gone. Kyle had backed off.

"Whoa! WAIT!" Harrison shouted, running toward the stage. "What happened to the door in the crotch?"

Shara gave a startled glance. "Harrison?"

"Hoo boy . . ." Casey said.

"Um, we changed the blocking," Dashiell explained.

"It wasn't reading from the audience," Mr. Levin said. "Also Kyle got a little . . . hurt the first time."

"No! Let me show you. It's a great slapstick bit if you do it right," Harrison said, jumping onstage. "Here's how you protect yourself."

Harrison ran through the scene, cheating with his hands as he turned so that the car door actually hit his palms first but appeared to smack him hard below the waist.

"Yeow," Reese said. "That could have serious consequences."

"Dude, you're a genius," Kyle said. "But, what are you doing here? Aren't you, like, banished?"

"I'm just here for a minute," Harrison explained.

"Let's attempt Harrison's blocking," said Dashiell eagerly. "And, Harrison, if you could spare just a few nanoseconds more, we could also use some assistance with the scene before 'Magic Changes'— "

Harrison shook his head. "Nahh, I can't . . . I have to be at the diner for a five o'clock shift."

Kyle glanced at the clock. "It's three fifty-seven. You have some time."

"I promised Dad. We have a deal. But I guess just one time through . . ."

"Well, anyone asks me, I didn't see a thing," Kyle said softly.

"Me neither," Reese added.

Harrison looked tentatively at Mr. Levin. "I'm, um, going to get a cup of coffee," Mr. Levin said. "Coming, Ms. Gunderson?"

She glanced up from the piano, where she was notating music. "Huh? Oh! Yes, right, coffee. Peter will play."

As they walked out, Dashiell announced in a soft voice, "People, for the next half hour, please give Harrison as much generous undivided attention as you have been giving me. Me, I'm heading back to the projection booth for a conference."

Harrison took a deep breath. They were all looking at him expectantly.

He had made a vow to himself. No *Grease*.

The deal had been clear in Harrison's mind, and he had stuck to it. Hoping that, at the very least, his father would catch so much crap from everyone—and feel so guilty—that he would never again even dream of interfering with Harrison's acting. But the deal meant *not* doing stuff like this.

Still. They needed him. Now that he was here, if he said no, that would really suck.

"Okay, first," Harrison said, "let's take apart the lead-in to 'Magic Changes'—Burger Palace Boys, where are you? Try this—let's run the lines doublespeed, just to pick up the cues."

The guys jumped in, racing through the lines. Then,

when they ran them at normal speed, the lines were crisper and funnier. Harrison sat through the choreography, then directed Kyle on his Act Two lines. He worked with Chip on voice projection. With Aisha on her New York accent. With Sammy, who was still hoarse, on vocal projection for "Beauty School Dropout."

The results were amazing. Except for Sammy, who seemed to have a major voice problem, they all improved. Harrison hadn't felt this alive in weeks. "The play is going to be *great!*" he shouted. "Now quick, let's do the opening scene—"

He glanced at the clock. It was 5:07.

"*DAMN,*" he shouted. "Never mind—gotta go! Bye."

He turned downstage and ran up the aisle. At the division between the front and back of the auditorium he took a hard right toward the door.

A large, familiar figure stood just inside, leaning against the wall with his arms folded.

Harrison stopped short. "Dad!" he squealed. "Yeah . . . I'm late . . . I was just going . . ."

He shut up. He was dead meat.

Mr. Michaels gave him a long, hard look. He gestured with his head, then walked out into the lobby.

Harrison followed him.

They walked out of school and into the van. Then they drove, without a word, to Kostas Korner.

33

Tuesday, February 12, 7:09 P.M.
dramakween: *o god casey i feel so nervous*
changchangchang: y?
dramakween: *theyre gonna hate me*
dramakween: *for doing that stupid thing at the beach*
dramakween: *theyre gonna look at me like i totally lost it like im crazy*
changchangchang: nobody thinks that, bri
dramakween: *maybe i should switch schools*
changchangchang: after the show, ok? lol we already lost a danny
changchangchang: & theres no female equivalant of a kyle in rhs

changchangchang: & we're gonna have the 1st musical rehearsal this wk, w peter mansfield & the orchestra.

changchangchang: besides they will b so happy 2 see u, theyre planning a little party at the rehearsal but i wasnt suposed 2 tell

dramakween: *really???? that is so sweet*

changchangchang: so dont worry, harrison is the one who should worry, his dad caught him coaching scenes at today's rehearsal.

dramakween: *oh god hes dead.*

"He must have killed you," said Brianna.

"He didn't say anything," Harrison said, holding the auditorium door open for Brianna. She looked great, he thought. It was her first day back, and he'd convinced her to meet Kyle onstage for a brushup rehearsal during lunch period. "We haven't said a word since he told me I had to quit the play. Not one. When we went to Chicago he sat far away from me on the plane. At the diner he talks to Niko and Niko talks to me. It's like I don't exist. Except when he has to sneak around to spy on me. I don't know if he saw me rehearsing or not. But I'm not doing it again. Next time, he might bring a butcher knife."

"Please, Harrison . . ."

"So last night we just went to the diner, in total silence, and I did my shift. Then he drove me home. Not back to Craig's, but to our house. We listened to a Yanni CD. It was torture. Dad went right to bed and I had to walk to Craig's—but I couldn't go to sleep for hours."

"You should have called me," Brianna replied. "I was up doing homework."

Harrison raised an eyebrow. "Uh-huh . . ."

"Don't worry, Mom," Brianna said. "No supplements. Well, some jasmine tea."

As Brianna turned down the center aisle, Charles rushed up to her. "Welcome home, princess!" he said. "And on the occasion, an announcement. Your bustier is ready."

"Bustier? I'm wearing a bustier?"

"For Rizzo? Of course! You're a brazen hussy, dear." Charles folded his arms. "And do *not* give me a hard time on this one. Shara's complaining about an itchy cardigan and Reese wants a miniskirt! In the 1950s!"

"Okay, I love it, Charles!" Brianna said.

"That's better." Charles kissed her on the cheek. "I am *so* glad to see you. How are you feeling after our dip in the Atlantic?"

"Great. You?"

"I'm joining the swim team next year," he replied, running backstage.

Kyle was onstage, tinkering with Greased Lightning, which had been wheeled out to the center. "Yo, Brianna!"

He leaped off the stage, faltering on his ankle, and rushed over to her. "Man, I heard what you did. Was that because of me?"

"It was because of me," Brianna replied. "I'm okay, really."

"Harrison thinks you can do this—are you up for it? I

need a Shara stand-in. She has math this period. It's for the 'Drive-In Movie' scene. You basically get in the car and I try to feel you up and you slam the door on my—uh—privates."

"Sounds like fun," Brianna said.

Harrison handed her a script. As she hopped onstage, he took a seat near the front. From the wings came the rhythmic sound of a hand saw. Charlettes were buzzing around, putting fluorescent tape on the floor.

"I want to get the door slam right," Kyle said.

"Don't forget to shield yourself with your hands," Harrison replied.

"I don't need to," Kyle said with a triumphant smile. "I'm wearing a cup."

Brianna winced. "Uh, too much informaaaation . . ."

As they ran lines, Harrison watched closely. Kyle was fine throughout the scene. Except for the part where Danny forces a kiss on Sandy. But that wasn't Kyle's fault. "You're supposed to resist!" Harrison reminded her.

"Right . . ." Looking a bit dazed, Brianna broke loose and got out of the car. As Kyle lurched after her, across the car's front seat, she slammed the door.

Harrison flinched. The contact with Kyle's nether regions looked a little too real.

Kyle convulsed. His eyes bugged out. His mouth dropped open. He fell backward onto the car's front seat, his legs flying in the air, then launched himself into a somersault that lifted him up over the driver side of the car. He managed to fall on the floor and tumble forward, hitting the side of the proscenium arch and then doing a comic bounce-leap back to center stage, where he rolled over the hood of the car and crashed to the floor with a loud "Oof!"

It was so over-the-top. Way beyond what the script had said.

And brilliant.

The Charlettes burst into applause. Brianna was convulsed with laughter.

"Keep it, it's perfect!" Harrison said.

Kyle didn't respond. His face was red, his teeth clenched. He was clutching his right ankle with both hands. "*How'd . . . I do?*"

"Kyle?" Brianna said, running across the stage. "Are you hurt?"

"I . . . planned that whole thing. But it's . . . my ankle . . ."

Harrison jumped onto the stage. "Can you move it?"

"Aaaaaghhh!" Kyle said. "Yup. It's okay."

Charles ran in from the wings. He knelt down and hooked Kyle's arm around his shoulder. "Let's get him to the nurse's office. Please put 'Charles Scopetta, emergency services' in the program."

Harrison got the other arm and lifted Kyle off the ground. "I'll be okay," Kyle said through a grimace. "Feels like a sprain. I'm a jock. I know when it's bad. This is nothing. What'd you think? Of the scene?"

"It was great, Kyle," Harrison said, feeling all of Kyle's 210 pounds on his own shoulder. "But next time, for your own sake, tone it down."

Harrison's cell phone rang that night while he was emptying the dishwasher at the diner. He hated this job. The glasses and silverware were always scorchingly hot, and he had to sort the different size forks and spoons, which were hard to tell apart.

"'Sup?" he said, balancing the phone on his shoulder as he dropped the silverware in bins.

"Where are you?" Brianna voice asked. "We're waiting for you. By the window. Near the photo of you on the donkey when you were five. We're having a meeting here because we figured it was the only way you could join us."

"Table six?" A glass slipped out of Harrison's hand and smashed onto the floor. "Ah, crap, look what you made me do."

"*I don't know the table numbers, Harrison!* This is an emergency. We've been here for ages. It's broken, Harrison!"

"I know it's broken! I have to get a broom."

"*Kyle's ankle*, Harrison. It's broken. He can't perform."

"WHAT?" Harrison pulled a bar stool into a corner and sat. All of a sudden his head hurt.

"That's why we're here," Brianna replied. "We have to rework the schedule. Musical rehearsals begin tomorrow. Peter Mansfield needs to hear the cast. We have to get a new Danny. But I think we found one."

"Who?"

"*Who do you think?*"

"Devon?"

"Are you crazy? *You.*"

"Me what?"

"You're playing Danny."

Harrison closed his eyes. His head was pounding.

"Don't hang up, Harrison," Brianna said. "You're the only one. Think of it—who else?"

"I can't. You *know* I can't."

"Talk to your dad."

"I haven't talked to him in days. You know the drill. I talk to Mom, I talk to Niko. *They* talk to him."

"Beg him. Get down on your hands and knees and promise you'll take over the diner when you grow up—"

"I don't beg," Harrison said. "Ever. Especially to him."

"You are a stubborn jackass, Harrison. Always thinking of yourself! Will you come out here so we can talk in person?"

"Sorry, Brianna. I'm out. Totally out. I try to help, I get in trouble. My life really bites right now. It will only get worse if I let you suck me in."

"Harrison—"

"I'll get through this, and so will you. Good-bye."

"Harrison, don't hang up—"

Harrison clicked off the phone and put it in his pocket. The broom was hanging from a hook on the back wall. He lifted it off and turned toward the mess.

His father was standing just inside the kitchen, his fist against the doorjamb. "You talking to Brianna." A statement, not a question.

"Are you speaking to me?" Harrison said, starting to sweep. "Or is Niko here?"

"She have loud voice," his dad said. "I hear what she say."

Harrison didn't know if he meant overheard her in the diner or heard her through the phone. "It's none of your business, Dad."

"She right. You jackass."

"Great, Dad. That's helpful and supportive. Let's go back to not talking, okay?"

"Always thinking of *youself.*"

"You told me that already, but thanks a lot for the reminder." Harrison threw the broom down. He tried to reel his temper back but it was going, going, gone . . . "Where do you think I get it from? *Who do you think I take after?*"

His father moved forward, hands clenched by his side. "Is no good to let down you friends. The Spartiati—the soldiers from Sparti—they always help their friends. What you want to do, clean broken gless while you friends having beeg trouble?"

Harrison's mouth flopped open then shut. The words that had arranged themselves into a battalion suddenly fell apart. "What are you *talking* about, Dad?"

Mr. Michaels pounded the top of the dishwasher. "Two days ago I go to school, to get you when you late. I watch you working with actors. You tell them what to do. Like boss!" He pointed to his head. "You smart. You smarter than all of them. *All* of them!"

"What are you trying to tell me?"

"You supposed to *help* you friends! How many times I tell you?"

"But—but I thought—what about the forty days? The *mnimosino*? Respecting the dead? I *can't* help them!"

"You respect dead, Haralambos. All Greeks respect dead. But selfish? No having responsibility? How can you do thees?"

"But *you* were the one who told me I couldn't do it!"

"I no raise you to be selfish! I raise you to be man. To think like man. To always do what is right. If you no talk to Brianna, then I talk to her!"

With that, he turned and stomped out of the room.

Harrison sank back in the chair.

In a daze, he lifted the broom. He took a dustpan with his left hand. Very carefully, he swept the shards of broken glass into the bin and dumped them in a garbage pail.

Guillermo peeked in through the door. "What are you doing in here?"

"I just got yelled at by my dad," Harrison said. "He made no sense."

"You need to translate what he said, Harrison," Guillermo scolded.

"He was speaking English!"

"No, he wasn't." Guillermo smiled. "That was Dad language. Mine spoke it, too. It means 'I'm sorry.' Now get the hell out of there before he changes his mind!"

Harrison smiled.

All bets were off, then. He did not need a second invitation.

He went into the dining room at a run.

Part 4
We Go Together

March 21

34

!!TONIGHT!!!

The Annual Ridgeport High Musical

Grease!

Tickets **SOLD OUT**

<u>Standby List</u> posted on School Office Door

Room 123

"Hold still," said Charles, staring past Harrison's face into the Green-Room mirror.

Harrison closed his eyes. He couldn't look. His hair had too much gel and resembled a pile of soggy black spaghetti. "I look like hell. I can barely remember my lines, I never was a good dancer, and now my good looks are gone."

"Modest as always," Brianna remarked, putting on her curly brunette wig.

"You talk too much," Charles said, struggling with Harrison's hair. "You fart too much. And you *move too much*! Hold still and I'll fix!"

"Who farts?" said Jamil, who was stretching on the floor. "I'll smack him."

"Can Peter Mansfield come in here?" Shara asked. "Would you guys mind if we had a short coaching session right now?"

"Mee-oh, mee-oh, mee-oh!" sang Reese, warming up. "Yuck. I sound terrible."

"You sound great," said Casey, who was posting the set change list onto the wall.

"*Reese, there are more important things to think about right now, like Danny Zuko's hair!*" Charles said. "Uch, Harrison, go wash that mess. We're going to start from scratch."

"Does this look hot or tacky?" Brianna asked, scrutinizing herself in a mirror. She was wearing a tight black skirt with a sweater that clung to her bustier. Her blond hair had been tucked under the short dark wig, and she had drawn a beauty mark on her left cheek.

"Yes," said Shara.

"That's what I wanted to hear," Brianna replied.

Chip, wearing thick horn-rim glasses, a checked shirt, and black-and-white saddle shoes, smiled at Casey. "You look beautiful."

"Thanks," Casey replied with a confused smile. "So do you."

Dashiell peeked in from the hallway. "Has anyone seen Sammy? He did not sign in."

"He was with Ms. Gunderson in the hallway," Brianna said. "Crying. He's getting cold feet. Doesn't want to be in the show. He's begging her to use a sub—*anyone*. Same old same old. He can talk fine, but for some reason he can't sing. I told you we should have replaced him."

"It's psychological," Dashiell said. "I'll talk to him about mind-body connectivity."

"That'll really pull him in," Reese said, pulling open her blouse just a couple of buttons too much.

"Oh, my heart—button up, this is *Grease*, not *Flashdance!*" Charles said, indignantly turning on the sink spigots.

"Break a leg, everyone!" Dashiell said. He gave Shara a quick kiss on the cheek and then left.

Charles raised an eyebrow. "Well."

"Goin' steady?" Brianna asked in her best Rizzo voice.

"Not me, I'm Sandra Dee," Shara replied, her face turning red.

"Harrison, I said get that schmutz out of your hair!" Charles commanded.

"Yes, sir." Harrison raced out of the Green Room, heading for the bathroom in a gale of laughter.

"Good evening, ladies and gentleOOOOOOOOOO!"

As Dashiell pulled back the mike, Casey covered her ears. Feedback was not cool. Ripley had had plenty of time to work that out.

" . . . uh, gentlemen," Dashiell continued. "I'm Dash Hawkins, and a hearty welcome from staff and thespians, to the annual Ridgeport High School Spring Musical!"

"BOOOOYAHHHH!" A cheer boomed from the back of the house.

The track team. Which was basically most of the football team. Casey glanced among them for Kyle, but it was dark and she couldn't quite make him out.

Reese smothered Casey in a hug. She was crying. "You're the best stage manager ever and I love you!"

Casey gently buttoned Reese's top shirt button. "You are hot. Frenchy is not."

" . . . Originally produced in Chicago in 1971," Dashiell intoned, reading from prepared notes, "*Grease* was originally meant to be a Vietnam-era commentary on Eisenhower-year sensibilities, a fact which is sometimes lost on twenty-first-century theatergoers . . ."

"Uh-oh," Aisha whispered. "We're dead."

"HEY, DADDY-O, PUT A LID ON THE FRABBAJABBA AND SCRAM!"

Harrison was onstage now, hips thrust forward, combing his hair and confronting Dashiell.

"Pardon me, I happen to be the student director," Dashiell said.

The crowd was giggling. Casey, too. This intro had been Harrison's last-minute idea.

"And I . . . am duh student EJECTOR!" Harrison said, lifting Dashiell onto his shoulders.

From the back of the auditorium came a thunderous laugh. "HAAAAHAHAHAHA!"

"Is that . . . ?" Reese asked.

Casey nodded. "God bless America . . ."

Onstage, Dashiell feigned shock, Harrison gave him a noogy on the head, and they both turned to the audience, smiling. "Ladies and gentlemen, presenting . . . *Grease!*"

Loud applause. It had worked. It was very clever.

Leave it to Harrison, Casey thought.

Peter Mansfield raised his baton and the orchestra started.

Casey's heart felt like it was going to break through her chest. Her eyes began seeing spots. She felt as if she wanted to throw up. She didn't think she could move. And she wasn't even going onstage.

By opening curtain, Charles wanted to kill Gabe for adding a motor to the car, which went off all by itself as the cast were taking their places.

By the first musical number, he wanted to kill the cast.

By the start of the second act, he wanted to kill himself.

These were excellent signs.

The wish for mass murder, he had come to realize, was healthy in the theater, as long as one refrained from the accomplishment thereof.

He stood calmly in front of the Green-Room door. *No one allowed.* By order of Dashiell and Mr. Levin.

"Charles, where's my lead pipe?" Barry demanded, running back from stage left.

"Where I told you it was," Charles replied, "where it has been since day one, if you had been listening. In the prop room, second to bottom shelf, left-hand side."

"Okay," Barry said, rushing away.

Charles sighed. *They take you for granted all through the rehearsals. They never listen. And then, during the show, when they're supposed to know . . .*

Now it was Reese's turn. Adjusting her bright red Frenchy wig, she scurried up to him urgently. "Where *is* he?" Reese hissed.

"He? I'm not in charge of personnel, only inanimate objects," Charles said, fixing her blouse, which had somehow once again become unbuttoned a bit too far.

She slapped his hand aside. "The next scene is 'Beauty School Dropout' *and we have no Teen Angel!* Where's Sammy?"

"Our Teen Angel is preparing in the Green Room," Charles replied calmly. "He requires a moment of rest. Have no fear. Places for Scene Two, toots."

Charles grinned as he watched Reese stomp back to stage right.

Knock, knock, knock. "Clear, please!" came a voice from behind the Green-Room door.

Charles smiled and pulled it open.

Out walked an outrageous-looking Elvis impersonator. His hair had been brushed into an impossible upsweep and he wore a white sequined outfit that had been inspired by Elvis, fitted to Sammy, and somehow taken out at least three sizes. Unlike Elvis, however, he used a crutch for walking.

"You look fabulous, Kyle," Charles said, "and they will plotz when they see you. But you're late. Now sit!"

Two Charlettes rolled a wheeled stool toward Kyle.

"Mi-mi-mi," Kyle sang, sitting on the stool and handing Charles the crutch. A huge smoke effect, wafting across the stage, began seeping slowly around the edges of the curtains.

"Go," Charles said. "NOW!"

He ran around into the wings to watch. In the midst of the smoke, as a cast of singing angels fluttered onto the stage, the Charlettes rolled Kyle on.

As the smoke cleared, revealing Kyle, the audience gasped. Then they broke into wild applause.

Charles watched Reese. She couldn't have done a better double take if she'd been coached.

He glanced out into the audience. At the end of the first row, Sammy grinned and gave him a thumbs-up.

"You sneak," Casey whispered in his ear. "Why didn't you let us tell them?"

Charles smiled. "We are here, darling, to create moments."

Backstage, Harrison couldn't stop giggling.

Kyle was amazing. With Sammy's desperate encouragement over the last two days, Harrison had been trying to convince Kyle to do this part. It was only just before the show that Kyle had agreed.

It was a brilliant move. Kyle's ovation was deafening.

Even immobile, even sitting in a chair, he could bring the house down.

And now, Harrison thought, *it's my turn.*

Waiting for his cue, he ran onstage. The lead-in to "Drive-In Movie." The car scene.

He had the blocking in his blood. The laughs were there. Shara was perfect. Prim and virginal and shocked. As she ran out of the car, Harrison prepared for the slam. He had rehearsed it to death at home. He lunged after her.

And slipped.

As he fell into the car seat, the door swung toward his face.

Shara screamed.

The pain ripped through him. Harrison felt as if he'd lost his nose.

Don't think. DON'T. THINK.

"NYAAHHOOOWWWW . . ." Harrison grabbed his nose and stood up. He looked at the audience, and let whatever was in his brain come out his mouth. "CCCHHHHTHHAAAACHHHH . . ."

They were laughing.

He fell over the side of the car and slid down the trunk. He landed in a near split on the floor.

He checked the inside of his palm. No blood. Good.

He cupped his hands over his nose in a prayer shape, hiding the nose completely. Then he dug his thumbnails, hidden by his hands, under his front teeth. Jerking his cupped hands to the right, he pulled his thumbnails forward so they made a snapping noise against his teeth.

It was a corny old trick. It sounded like he was breaking a bone in his nose—or setting it back in place. The body mike was a huge help—it sounded like he had cracked his skull.

A big groan swept across the audience.

He let go and forced a smile. "Dat's bettuh!" he said.

And then, as Harrison stood with a triumphant smile, they burst into applause. His dad, sitting in an aisle seat, looked totally bewildered. Concerned.

Mansfield was smiling. He would make the orchestra vamp until the audience stopped.

Harrison turned and gave them all a big wink. They cheered again. His dad was on his feet, beaming with pride.

Harrison felt good. He had the audience in his pocket.

Where they belonged.

35

"AMAZING!" CHARLES SCREAMED. HE WASN'T supposed to be onstage after the final curtain call—and neither were the other Charlettes. They had work to do. But the curtain had been left open, per the plan, for a wild impromptu fifties dance. Audience members were jumping onstage. Vijay's grandmother was doing the Lindy with his little sister. Kyle was doing wheelies in the wheelchair the Drama Club had used in 1985 for *The Man Who Came to Dinner*. And Reese was standing center stage in the middle of it all with a camera, taking photos of the audience.

"They *LOVED* us!" Brianna shouted, jumping into Harrison's arms.

Harrison swung her around and planted a big fat kiss on her lips.

"OOH-LA-LA!" bellowed Mr. Michaels from the auditorium.

"He notices everything, doesn't he?" Brianna said.

Harrison smiled. "Just wait till I start kissing the guys."

"Thank you for coming, ladies and gentlemen, and please stay for refreshments in the gym—and a real sock hop, led by Mansfield and the Marauders!" Mr. Levin shouted into a mike before Ms. Gunderson pulled him away to dance a jitterbug.

Chip was doing a prim little dance with Casey. Dashiell was flailing wildly, a spare tire from Greased Lightning hanging around his neck, causing Shara to laugh so hard she couldn't move. Sammy was hand-jiving his way through the crowd. He gave Kyle a hug, pointed to his own throat—and then, with a big smile, silently mouthed, "Thank you."

Kyle pulled him into his lap and wheeled them both, soundlessly screaming, through the dancing crowd.

"LET'S BLOW THIS POP STAND!" shouted Mr. Ippolito, walking the hot rod off the stage and wearing a garish rhinestone-studded white leather jacket.

Chip held his arm out to Casey. "May I?"

"Is this a date?" Casey asked.

"Jeepers, yes," Chip replied.

"Gag me," said Casey with a grin as they walked off.

Dashiell flung aside the tire and put his arm around Shara. "Well?"

Shara smiled and stood on tiptoes to give him a chaste kiss on the cheek. "Sure, Dash."

"*Dash!*" Dashiell said, pumping his fist in the air. "*She calls me Dash!*"

"Oh, the drama," Charles said. "I can't stand it. Harrison, turn, please . . ."

Harrison grinned. Arms around Brianna, he looked out into the crowd one last time.

A flash went off. Mr. Michaels put down his bulky old film camera and, with a wide grin, gave his son a theatrical thumbs-up.

Harrison returned it. "Ooh-la-la."

"Shall we?" Brianna said. "The sock hop is starting without us."

Turning upstage, Harrison put his free arm around Charles.

The three of them walked out the rear stage door, arm in arm, singing at the top of their lungs.

Mr. Michaels's flash went off again, behind them. "God bless America," he shouted, "and my son Haralambos!"

Epilogue

OKAY, I KNOW YOU'RE WONDERING.

Even if you're not, I'll tell you.

I got a 2320. On the SATs.

Don't hate me. Charles already does. He says he will never, ever worry about me again. Harrison thinks I should offer to spread my excess points to the other DC members.

He didn't do so bad either. But he won't tell me the score. I just know, because his dad keeps saying, "My son is GENIUS!"

Of course, he could be talking about the show. Mr. Michaels loved it. My mom said he was crying afterward. Crying is not the usual reaction to *Grease*, but who knows. (Dad says he may have been crying out of deep

· 222 ·

disappointment, because he thought the show was about Greece. But that's my dad's humor. Or what passes for it.)

Everyone said it was the best Spring Musical ever. The people who remember the *Grease* from the 1980s claimed that show didn't compare to ours. Then again, everyone always says that kind of thing.

But I believe it. People will never stop talking about Harrison's last-minute Danny. Kyle's fall and rise and fall. And rise. His surprise entrance as Teen Angel.

I'll never forget this play either. Well, the last part of it. The part that happened after the beach.

I don't remember much about what happened before. I was kind of dead to the world. I guess I let things get out of hand.

Dad and Mom talked to me a lot. And they supported me when I dropped the SAT review class. I guess I might have done a little better had I stayed, but I'm happy.

Devon Roper hasn't said a word to me. I think he feels guilty. I think he feels responsible for my wigging out at the beach. I see him skulking around the side of the school. I say hi, but he doesn't respond much.

So it's the final push to the end of the year. College visits, another few months of Mr. Brotman, but unfortunately, no more plays.

As for Harrison, well, we're pals again. But it's more than that now. I think we both realize it. Still, we're both being really cautious.

There's a saying in the theater world. Never get involved with someone in the same show. It ruins everything.

I think we both know that.

But honestly, I'm leaving the possibility open. At least until after the next play.

And there will be another one, maybe this summer. After all, this is Ridgeport.

Whenever it is, Harrison will be in it. And I will be getting peaceful sleep.

Maybe the bad dreams will ease up by then. I've been having them a lot. Waves, sand, cold rocks.

I still don't know quite what came over me. Till the day I die, I will never forget what Charles and Casey did.

Well, maybe I will. But it doesn't matter. If all else fails, I know one thing for sure.

Charles will remind me.